A Long Way Home

To the Vermont Studio Center
with thanks for helping
to make this book possible.

Nancy Price Graff

A Long Way Home

NANCY PRICE GRAFF

Clarion Books
New York

Clarion Books
a Houghton Mifflin Company imprint
215 Park Avenue South, New York, NY 10003
Copyright © 2001 by Nancy Price Graff

The text was set in 11-point Garamond.

www.houghtonmifflinbooks.com

Printed in U.S.A.

Library of Congress Cataloging-in-Publication Data

Graff, Nancy Price, 1953-
A long way home / by Nancy Price Graff.
p.   cm.
Summary: After moving to his mother's small hometown in Vermont, twelve-year-old Riley
must reconsider his feelings about war and heroes when he meets a man who refused to
fight in Vietnam and make a discovery about one of his own relatives.
ISBN 0-618-12042-4
[1. Moving, Household—Fiction. 2. Courage—Fiction. 3. War—Fiction. 4. Vermont—Fiction.]
I. Title.
PZ7.G75158 Lo 2001   [Fic]—dc21   2001028290

HAD   10 9 8 7 6 5 4 3 2 1

For my daughter, Lindsay,
who has Vermont in her bones

Acknowledgments

This is a work of fiction, and the people, places, and situations are all figments of my imagination. Although he knew nothing about it during its writing, this novel would never have been written without Ray, whom I love and hope to honor with this story. I would like to thank Karen Price Stewart and Charlotte MacLeay for reading an early draft. My son, Garrett, whose passion for the Civil War took us to Gettysburg when he was only eight, offered helpful advice about the war and chess. Howard Coffin read the parts about Gettysburg and made numerous suggestions, although if any errors appear, they are mine alone. My grandfather, Harper Alden Price, gave me the Civil War binoculars that hang in my kitchen. The Vermont Studio Center provided me with a room and the opportunity to write, for which I am grateful. I cannot thank Katherine Paterson enough for her encouragement, laughter, and sensitivity. Through her I met my editor, Virginia Buckley, who did not shy away from a complex manuscript but helped me make it clearer. Thank you. Thank you, also, to Jennifer Greene for her attention to the manuscript. Finally, I want to thank my husband, Chris, who has read almost every word I have ever written, given good counsel, and pushed me to keep going. My debt to him is beyond measure.

❧ *Chapter* ONE

Riley tried to push past the throng of screaming children at the doorway. Even from inside the school he could see his grandfather's big old brick house. Correction: *my* house, he thought grimly. It could not have been more than fifty yards away, but at that moment, caught in a sea of shrieking first and second graders greeting their mothers at the end of the first day of school, he was trapped. And so he waited to be carried forward by their enthusiasm for freedom after a day stuck indoors sitting on chairs when every person in his right mind would rather be anyplace but here.

At last he reached the sunlight, blindingly bright on the expanse of asphalt that dominated the front of the school. He stood there for one moment, blinking.

Wham! Someone plowed into him and nearly knocked him off his feet. The two books he had been holding went flying.

"Watch out, you idiot!" someone yelled at him too late.

It took a second for him to catch his breath and figure out what had just happened.

A handful of big boys, boys he recognized from his own seventh grade classes, were playing pavement hockey. The boy who had just run into him and who at this minute was running after the loose puck, as if he hadn't just about killed Riley, was Tim. Riley remembered his name—at least, his first name—from math and social studies. How could anyone forget him? He was the kid who sat in the back row making wisecracks until Mr. Aja, the social studies teacher, had finally ordered him to put all four legs of his chair on the floor, his hands on his desk, and a sock in his mouth.

Tim didn't seem the least bit sorry that Riley's English book was now lying splayed on the blacktop, one of its corners soaking up water from a small puddle. His math book lay askew, its spine clearly broken.

Criminy, Riley fumed as he picked up the books and felt the pockmarks the grit had made in their plastic covers. These books were shabby enough already compared to the ones in his old school, and he hadn't even gotten them home yet to cover with grocery bags, the way every teacher ordered every year.

"Watch out yourself," he muttered. It was obviously too late to offer a good retort; Tim was halfway across the parking lot by now, still moving like a runaway train. As Riley walked around the perimeter of the asphalt, he kept his eye on the game. The boys were flailing their sticks and chasing the puck as if they were chickens with their heads cut off, totally oblivious of the safety of small children and distracted mothers.

Somebody could get really hurt, he said to himself as he reached the safety of his grandfather's yard and began to cross the few yards of grass to the corner of the house. He thought of going to the front door, but in all his years of visiting his grandfather he had never seen anyone use the front door. Maybe it didn't even open. Even as a little kid, he'd noticed that nobody in Vermont used their front doors.

He had just reached the corner when he heard the crash of shattering glass. He whirled around in time to see the hockey players scattering like rabbits and disappearing behind the school, behind fences, behind rows of bushes, dragging their hockey sticks after them like stiff tails. In the amount of time it took Riley to find the gaping hole in one of the nine small panes that made up the ancient dining room window, all of the hockey players had disappeared.

"Mom, Mom!" he called, sprinting around the end of the house and up the porch steps to the back door.

Riley found his mother standing in the dining room, her hands on her hips and tears swimming in her eyes.

"Look at this," she said, waving a hand vaguely at the shards of splintered glass glistening on the floor.

"I know what did it," Riley volunteered.

"That's no mystery," his mother said as she leaned over and picked up a black hockey puck.

"No, I mean I know *who* did it," he corrected himself. "Well, sort of. They're in my class. At least, one of them is. His name is Tim. He just about killed me after school. They were playing hockey in the parking lot, but they all disappeared when the window broke."

His mother sighed and looked at the puck in her hand. She had deep blue shadows under her eyes, and her skin stood out pale against the freckles spangled across her nose and cheeks. Riley had those same freckles and the same light brown hair. His mother used the back of her other hand to sweep her hair out of her face. After a pause to collect herself, she turned to face him.

"Well, aside from this, how was your first day at the Sharon Consolidated School?" She gave him the best smile she could manage at that moment.

"Awful, just as I thought it would be," he said and immediately regretted it.

Riley waited for his mother to tell him that it couldn't have been *that* bad, that he couldn't expect much better if that was his attitude, but to her credit, she said nothing.

Instead, she walked toward him and put her arm around his shoulders. He was almost as tall as she was. Soon, he realized, she wouldn't be able to do that.

"You're going to have to give it some time. This is a small town, and it's pretty tightly closed against strangers. But you're not really a stranger—you've been coming here all your life. It's bound to crack somewhere and let you in," she said. Riley could hear the tiredness in her voice. "I'm sorry you're so unhappy, but for right now I think this is what's best for us." Her tone brightened. "How about running out to the car and bringing in the paint I bought today? The sooner we start making some improvements around here, the sooner it's going to feel like home."

This place is about as ready to crack open for me as a chunk of granite, Riley thought as he walked back outside to the faithful old blue station wagon. And this house will never be home. It's Grandpa's house, not mine.

Standing beside the car, he noticed for the first time how clear and sharp the day was, the kind of late summer day in Vermont when the fragrance of ripening apples and moldering flowers fills the air like an over-powering perfume. He stood there, conscious of the drone of bees working over the crab apples rotting under the tree nearby and the bulbous white clouds scudding across the sky. It is pretty here, he admitted reluctantly to himself, but that was the only thing Vermont had going for it over Stony Point, where he used to live.

"I hate it here," he said out loud. Then he leaned over and grabbed the wire handle on one of the gallons of paint. The weight of the can surprised him, and he winced as the handle bit into his fingers.

He didn't see how his mother could do it. There was so much work to be done on his father's house, and paint alone wouldn't begin to touch the real problems, like a kitchen floor so warped that peeling linoleum tripped everyone who tried to cross it, and bathroom plumbing so leaky that water had left webs of cracks in the ceilings downstairs.

He grabbed the second can of paint and staggered up the back steps, across the porch, and into the kitchen, while the handles threatened to amputate his fingers. As he put the cans down, he noticed the name of the color scrawled in black marker on each lid: "Lookin' Good Peach." Riley's eyes took in the dilapidated cupboards, the stained porcelain sink, the peeling floor, and he said to himself, There isn't enough paint in the entire world—in peach or any other color—to make this place look good.

Later, when he was upstairs in his room, he could hear his mother downstairs breaking the rest of the glass in the pane to neaten the edges. In a few minutes she came upstairs and asked Riley if he had the duct tape. She needed it, she said, to tape a cardboard patch into the broken window. When she left, he asked her to close the door behind her so he could be alone. He felt guilty about not helping, but he pushed away the voice that kept telling him this wasn't easy for her either. Let her suffer a little, too, he thought, although heaven knows, she's already suffered plenty. We both have.

Eventually, he took out his chess set and set up the pieces. He moved a white pawn and began playing a game. White pawn, black pawn. White pawn, black bishop. The game began to take shape. From the open window came the sound of young children screaming with delight on the playground at the school.

"Jeez!" he said. "Look at me! Two weeks ago I had friends. I had shopping centers. New York City was only forty-five minutes away. We took field trips every year to the Statue of Liberty and the Museum of Natural History to see the dinosaurs. I had a big middle school, and I was going to have Mrs. Stocek, the best science teacher in the whole school. I had Luke to play chess with, for crying out loud!" With the palm of his hand he swept all the remaining pieces off the board and onto his bed. It wasn't as if he didn't know how the game would end. He was playing both sides. He knew exactly how it was going to end, because that was the way he had set it up to end. Any moron could figure that one out.

"Riley?" His mother tapped lightly on the door. "We need milk for supper. How about walking down to the store with me? We can pick up the mail while we're there."

"And the mailman brought the mail right to the house

and put it in the box by the front door!" he announced loudly as he yanked his bedroom door open. He looked into his mother's startled face. "We didn't have to go down to the stupid general store or the post office or whatever else it is to pick up the mail!"

⚔ ⚔ ⚔

The Sharon General Store was less than a quarter of a mile away. Every time Riley saw the name Sharon, he thought with disgust that he had been forced to move to a town with a girl's name. Stony Point, his real home—back when he was happy, he reminded himself—had a nice ring to it. It suggested something solid and permanent, and it had always felt that way to Riley. But "Sharon" conjured up images of a skinny girl with long kinky hair, loopy earrings, wire-rimmed glasses, and one of those bright Indian skirts his mother still had hanging in her closet, even though it was 1980 and that style had gone out ten years ago. Of course, he had to be careful about the wire-rimmed glasses part, because he wore them, too, glasses that magnified his eyes and gave his face a look of perpetual wonder, people said. He could still remember the years of teasing he had endured because of them. Nobody in Stony Point teased him anymore about the glasses—maybe he had just gotten too big—but he was still sensitive about them.

Riley and his mother walked diagonally across the town green, following a path that had been worn bare by generations of the town's residents taking shortcuts across its grass. The green sloped gently downward toward town and was as big as a football field, with the old white courthouse at one end and the old white Congregational Church at the other, both of them with wide granite steps and thin spires piercing the sky. They looked alike in almost every other way, too, as far as Riley was concerned. Riley's grandfather's big brick house, close to 150 years old, the one he and his mother had just moved into two weeks ago, sat off to the side of the courthouse and no more than the throw of a softball from the town's consolidated school.

Sharon had seemed very different to Riley when he was much younger and had come up to visit his grandfather. Most of the residents lived back in the hills, many on dirt roads that snaked past abandoned pastures now overgrown with trees. The town itself was at the bottom of a narrow valley, laid out along what Riley had long thought was a river but that he now knew was just a sorry excuse for a stream. The town didn't pretend to much. It was about three blocks long, what his grandfather called "just a wide spot in the road." And everyone knew everyone else—and their business, too, his grandfather had warned. Sharon had seemed comfortable then because it was small and self-contained, like a cocoon, and so different from his home in Stony Point. But now that Sharon was home, now that his grandfather had died and he and his mother had moved to Sharon to live in his grandfather's house, it struck him very differently. It struck him as about as far from anyplace he'd like to live as he could imagine.

"I'll get the few things we need, Riley, you get the mail," his mother said as soon as they had walked through the door of the general store. She veered left, and Riley wandered over to the motley collection of toys the store carried. Jacks. A Wiffle ball. Balloons. Decks of cards. This is pathetic, he decided for the umpteenth time. He turned his attention to the hunting and fishing department. Riley had loved coming to this old brick store, when his grandfather used to bring him down and give him a dollar to spend. With its faded sign and enormous plate-glass windows festooned with notices of auctions and lost dogs, the store carried a little bit of everything: soup and baked beans, milk and cheese, maple syrup, toys, ice cream, potato chips, hunting jackets in mottled green-and-brown camouflage, and hunting vests in fluorescent orange—depending, Riley guessed, on whether you wanted to do the shooting or be shot at—fishing poles, shiny aluminum lures and delicate flies, writing paper, candles, rubber boots, and garden seeds. You could live your whole life and never shop anywhere else than in this room, no bigger than half a basketball court, Riley thought. If you wanted to, that is.

When he was satisfied that he had seen everything there was to see—probably everything there would ever be to see—he walked down the aisle to the back of the store and went over to the mail window. It was where everyone in Sharon got their mail. He could see piles of newspapers and magazines and several bundles of letters, and he could hear rustling as someone moved around in back behind the ancient wooden letter sorter. He stood there studying the hand-scribbled names of every family in town, all laid out in a grid, one name per little box. He could see Griffin at the very end of the names, along with the names of half a dozen other families who had arrived in Sharon after the postmistress had completed her annual assigning of boxes to the town natives in alphabetical order.

"Excuse me," he said after a moment or two.

A head popped up behind the letter sorter and looked at him through the wooden grid.

"Can I help you?" the young man asked. He obviously wasn't Mrs. Benedict, the postmistress, who, privy as she was to all the town's business, had probably memorized Riley's name before he even arrived.

"I'd like the mail for Griffin. It's there on the end," Riley said, trying to be helpful.

The man came from behind the sorter.

"Who are you?" he asked.

"I'm Riley Griffin," Riley replied.

"Do you have some identification?"

"No," Riley said. He nearly snorted in surprise at the question. "Kate Griffin's my mom. We're living in my grandfather's house, next to the courthouse. I've been picking up the mail for two weeks and Mrs. Benedict always gives it to me."

"I'm sorry, but this is the United States mail, and I don't know you," the man said, though he didn't seem very sorry. "I can't give it to you unless you can prove you're who you say you are."

"How am I supposed to do that?" Riley exclaimed.

"I'd suggest you bring one of your parents along," the man said. Then he walked back behind the letter sorter and disappeared again from sight.

"I only have one," Riley said. It was the second time that afternoon he had spoken to a retreating back, and it just made him angrier. He stood there thinking that he could probably spit tacks, as his grandfather used to say. Then he turned on his heel and stalked off to find his mother.

She was talking to an elderly woman near the meat counter. "And this must be your son," the older woman said, turning toward Riley. "I was just telling your mother that she was like the prodigal daughter the way she's come back to Sharon after all these years."

Riley nodded, although he had no idea what she was talking about.

"Didn't you get the mail?" Riley's mother asked him as she glanced down at his empty hands.

He nearly shouted at her. "No!"

"What's wrong?" She turned first to the woman with whom she'd been having her conversation and said, "Excuse me." Then she turned back to Riley, studying his face. "You look furious. What happened?"

"He wouldn't give it to me," Riley said.

"Who's 'he'?" she asked.

"The man giving out the mail," Riley said.

"Oh, that would be Harold Harrington," the elderly woman volunteered. "Helen had to go to a funeral in Tunbridge."

Now Mrs. Griffin guided her son back to the counter that passed for a post office in Sharon.

"Pardon me!" Mrs. Griffin said.

The young man's head popped up again behind the letter sorter.

"I'd like our mail," she said emphatically. "You wouldn't give it to my son."

The young man walked forward to the counter. "Are you Mrs. Griffin?" he asked.

"I am," Riley's mother replied. "I am Kate Griffin, Wallace Long's daughter. And this is my son, Riley—Riley Griffin."

"Gosh, you sure look like your father," the clerk said, staring at her. "I'm sorry about his passing. I've been at my folks' camp all summer. I hadn't heard you were going to move into your dad's old house."

"Well, we're going to give it a try. And Riley will be picking up the mail."

To need your mother to pick up the mail! Riley felt as if he were five years old. He felt as if this entire conversation were going on right over his head, even though he was nearly as tall as both of them. He wanted to crawl into one of those camouflage outfits hanging on the wall and disappear. His hands clenched and unclenched in his jeans pockets, and bright hot color spread from his neck to the tips of his ears, burning against the collar of his shirt.

"Well, all right," the young man said, looking from Riley's mother to Riley and back again. He reached behind him and took two letters from the slot and handed them to her. "You understand that we can't give mail to just anyone."

"I understand," Mrs. Griffin said, but Riley wished she had said other things to the young man.

They paid for the milk and some hamburger for dinner and headed silently back across the green. Riley could feel the evening air getting cooler. He shivered a little and hugged the bag of groceries closer for warmth until he felt the coldness of the carton of milk penetrating his shirt. He knew it would not have been this cold during the first week of September in Stony Point. He would not have needed his mother along to get the mail. He would not have been made a fool of after school, as he was today.

"I hate this place," Riley said.

"It's going to take some time to settle in," his mother said quietly.

❧ *Chapter* TWO

One week into the school year, Riley knew two things: He'd have no trouble getting straight A's, and he had made no friends at all—that is, if you didn't count Claire, a dark, sad-eyed second grader with coal-black hair whom he had knocked down one day as all thirteen grades were making their mad rush through the door at the end of school. It had been an accident, of course. He had thought—mistakenly, it turned out—that he had heard someone calling his name, and when he turned eagerly in the direction of the sound, his books had clipped her on the side of the head. She didn't cry. He had apologized and helped her up while the throng of bodies surged around them as if Riley had been Moses parting the seas.

He thought at first that he had caused her to tear the knees of her pants on the asphalt, but she assured him very solemnly that they were that way when she got them. So all he had to do was brush grit off the palms of her hands and flatten a drawing that had been wrinkled in the accident.

He studied the drawing for a moment. He felt he had to. Someone's dirty footprint had permanently spoiled it, and he was responsible.

"It's a fwog," she told him.

It took him a few seconds to figure out what she was saying.

"And that's the castle where the pwincess lives."

Then Riley could see the blond princess leaning out of the castle window with her stick-figure arms and her overly large hands with the fingers splayed out like the points of a star.

"I'm sorry about the dirt," he said when he was certain he had brushed off as much of it as he could.

"That's okay. Mawy won't mind," she assured him, and he smiled without having any idea who Mawy was.

"My name is Riley," he told her.

"Wiley," she said.

"No, Riley," he repeated slowly and more clearly.

She nodded. "Wiley." Then she told him her name, and once he had inserted an "r" where he knew one should be, he knew that her name was Claire. He had said that he would watch to make sure that she made it down and across the green without any more accidents.

She never smiled, not once, but as she went off down the green, she turned after every twenty or thirty steps and waved at him, until she was finally out of sight behind the laundromat at the far corner.

After that, Claire made a point of walking out with him every afternoon. She always seemed pleased to see him, certainly more pleased than he was to be leaving school every afternoon with a seven-year-old girl, but she never smiled. She just walked quietly beside him and then asked if he was going to watch her while she crossed the green. What could he say?

Fortunately, she didn't turn around every ten seconds now. She stopped only at the corner of the laundromat to wave once, and then Riley sprinted home.

Halfway through the second week of school, Riley came around the back corner of the house and spotted a faded red pickup truck parked in the driveway. It had a missing hubcap, and various dents and bruises indicated where it had come in contact with hard objects. Rust rose in graceful arches above the wheel wells like rainbows.

His mother was standing in the dining room talking to someone. Riley could hear the end of her story about how his father and baby sister had been killed in a car crash more than ten years ago. He knew the story well. Although he had been too young at the time to remember much, he had heard her tell the story over the years. He knew every detail. He knew the color of the car that had hit them and he knew how fast it had been going when it crossed the center line of the wet highway near their house one night.

The man in the dining room with Riley's mother was tall and stooped. He stood as if he had already worked a hard day, and his long face was drawn, but his dark gray eyes and the smile he was directing at Riley's mother were warm. He had a full head of thick brown hair that fell over his ears like the mane of hair that Jesus wore in most of the pictures Riley had seen of him. His carpenter's pants, full of pockets and strange loops and stained at the knees, hung on him, and the fingers of the hands that hung at his sides were long and unexpectedly delicate. Prayer hands, Riley decided, probably just like Jesus had.

"Riley," his mother said in a tone of voice slightly higher than the one she usually used. "Meet Sam. Sam is going to fix the broken windowpane."

Sam stuck out his prayer hand, and Riley had no choice but to offer him a hand in return.

"Sam, this is my son, Riley," his mother said.

"Mr.?" Riley asked, waiting for a last name.

"Just call me Sam. That's what everyone who speaks to me calls me. I've been hearing about you," Sam said, immediately making Riley worry about what his mother had been saying.

"You're tall for your age," Sam continued. "Play basketball?"

"No." Riley cut him off short. He was tired of the world assuming that if you're tall, you play basketball.

"How do you like school?" Sam asked, as if he hadn't noticed Riley snapping at him.

"I don't very much," Riley confessed. "At least, not so far."

"I never liked it much either," Sam admitted. "It wasn't the right place for me a lot of the time."

"Did you go to school here?" Riley asked, the question provoked by the way Sam rolled his head in the direction of the Sharon Consolidated School, which was so close it obscured any other view from the window.

"Sam and I went to school together, Riley," his mother volunteered. "Sam was two years ahead of me."

"Those two years made a world of difference. If I'd been in your class, the draft would have been almost over by the time I graduated. Maybe my chances would have been better." Sam laughed, but even though Riley didn't understand what Sam was saying, he could tell there wasn't anything funny about what he'd said.

"I didn't know you had served in Vietnam," his mother said, her eyebrows furrowing in a way that Riley recognized from times when he'd almost hurt himself doing something his mother thought was foolish.

Cool, Riley thought. His mind raced trying to imagine this lanky stranger dressed in fatigues and carrying a rifle through the vast rice paddies he'd seen in pictures.

"Briefly." Sam laughed again, the same inscrutable sound that indicated neither amusement nor pleasure. "Might even have set a record for brevity. At least, that's what some of the folks think around here."

He turned to Riley.

"I'm going to fix the window. Want to help?"

Riley didn't particularly want to, but there wasn't any polite way out of it, and besides, he didn't have anything else to do or anyone else to do it with.

"Sure. Why not?" he shrugged. "What do you want me to do?"

✂ ✂ ✂

Riley would have found something else to do if he had realized when he accepted Sam's invitation that it meant standing outside, in the front yard, where everyone could see him.

"This is tough, old hardwood. It's been here a long time, probably since the house was built," Sam said as they struggled to remove the wood frame from the brick box in which it was trapped. Using crowbars and screwdrivers, they finally pried off the casing and freed the window. Sam held it up to the light.

"See those waves?" Sam asked as he held up the frame containing the eight remaining panes of glass, each of them about the size of his hand.

Riley could see in each pane a swirl of movement, as if the glass were flowing like a curving river.

"What is that?" Riley asked. He looked from one pane to the next. For the first time he noticed how the world beyond the glass swam in front of his eyes as if riding the river. "Why does all the glass look like that?"

"When this house was built, molten glass was spun on a wheel into big sheets and then broken off into pieces to use in panes like these," Sam explained. "So each pane has a piece of the concentric circles as they spun out from the center, which was called the bull's-eye. And then they made one final pane out of the bull's-eye. That's what you have in the fanlight over your front door. They didn't waste anything."

Riley stepped back and looked at the row of six small panes that topped the front door. As he studied those dark green whorls, each nearly as fat as his fist in the middle, he followed the curves to the center, where all the spinning had started.

"I never knew that," Riley admitted. "That's really neat."

"I'll tell you, the world sure looks different through old glass. These old houses have a lot of stories to tell," Sam said as he removed the few remaining shards of glass from the wooden muntins dividing the panes. "It'll be a shame to have one pane in this beautiful set filled with ordinary modern glass, but there's no getting around that."

"I like history," Riley said. "It's my favorite subject."

"Is it?" Sam asked. "I never liked it when I was your age. I thought it was all about dead people I didn't care about. I look at it differently now that I spend a lot of my time working with old buildings."

"What did you like?" Riley asked.

"Me? Art. Art was all I cared about," Sam said, finishing the last bit of cleaning around the frame. "I lived and breathed art, and the school offered it twice a week. Mrs. Jersey came over from Tunbridge and gave us fat pencils and oak-tag paper and expected us to be creative."

Sam stood up.

"I'm going to throw this in my truck and take it to the shop," he said. "I'll have it back here in an hour or so. Maybe you can come back out then and help me put it in place."

While Sam was gone, Riley wandered inside for a snack. His mother was peeling old liner paper off the kitchen shelves.

"This stuff has been here for thirty or forty years," she complained, her red face a portrait of frustration. As Riley ate a cookie, he watched her jam a scraper under the paper edge and try to lift it off in one big sheet, but it shredded with age and clung to the shelf where it had lived for so many years, like a snake reluctant to come out of its hole.

"Who's Sam?" Riley asked.

"Oh, you wouldn't believe how crazy I was about him when I was in tenth grade and he was in twelfth." She stopped tugging and laughed. "He was tall, dark, and handsome, and I suffered the cruelest kind of schoolgirl crush."

"What happened?" Riley asked.

"He graduated and left Sharon. I lost track of him, which is how most schoolgirl crushes end," his mother said.

"Where did you run into him?" Riley asked.

"At the store," she said. "I had heard he was living back in the hills, and I intended to look him up, but then we were both in the store this morning and ran into each other. It turns out he's a carpenter, and I asked him if he could come fix the window before it starts to get cold at night."

A little more than an hour later Sam was back. Fifteen minutes after that, Sam and Riley had reinstalled the window. They stood back to admire their handiwork.

"That new pane looks ugly," Riley said, surprised to have an opinion about something he'd known nothing about two hours earlier.

"Yep, it does," Sam agreed. "But it will keep the cold out as well as the old ones. I'll keep an eye out on my jobs, and if I ever find one that matches the others, we'll replace it."

Riley's mother came outside to join them in the warm late-afternoon sun.

"How much do I owe you?" she asked Sam. She held her checkbook in her hand.

"Nothing," Sam said, bending over to put his tools back in his wooden tool chest.

"Oh, come on," Riley's mother protested. "I never meant for you to do the work for free."

"Nothing," Sam repeated. He stood up and smiled. "It was my pleasure. Welcome back."

"Well, then, you'll have to come to dinner. Can you come Friday night?" She blushed. "I never even asked you: Are you married? Do you have kids?"

"Nope, there's just me," Sam said, sounding embarrassed—or apologetic—as if he'd done something wrong.

"Please come," Riley's mother insisted. "And don't bring a thing."

✘ ✘ ✘

In bed that night, Riley studied the weird triangles and rectangles of light that came in through his window and fell on his ceiling and walls from the orange spotlight that illuminated the front of the school every night. The hardness of the light had bothered him for the first few nights, but he was surprised at how quickly he had grown used to it. It seemed to compensate for the loss of the familiar drone of Stony Point's traffic, for the Sharon silence, for the long nights as still and quiet as a cemetery. Now he adjusted his shade each night so that just enough light came in to keep him company. Tonight, for the first time, he noticed the undulating curves in the light on his walls, and he thought of the garish orange light passing through and being magnified by the wavy ancient glass in his old window.

As he did every night, he scrutinized the ceiling with special concentration. He did this partly out of curiosity but partly out of genuine concern. He was not yet convinced that the sagging plaster over his head would stay in the ceiling, where it belonged.

His mother's mention of the car crash had started him thinking about his father and his baby sister. He had only a few precious memories of his father, but he remembered well his father's laughter, which had filled the rooms of their house in Stony Point in a way that no sound since then ever had. He had even fewer memories of Cassie, but he could remember the peach fuzz on her head and how soft it felt against his chin when he held her, squirming, on his lap. He could remember her pink and moist from her bath, smelling of baby powder.

Before he closed his eyes, he said the prayer that he had started saying every night. For the most part he had stopped saying prayers when he finally realized that his father and sister were never going to be returned to him, regardless of how much he begged or promised God. But he still gave in from time to time when he felt the situation was desperate enough to warrant even the possibility of extra help. Sometimes he got what he wanted, and sometimes he didn't. He had no idea if God was responsible or not.

"Dear God," he whispered, "please make Mom change her mind. Please. I don't think that I can live here.

I think that I will die if you make me stay." Then because he thought it would sound better if God thought he was thinking of someone other than himself, he added, "And then Mom won't have anybody."

❧ *Chapter* THREE

Friday after school, Riley's mother sent him outside to work. He found himself in the front yard raking up drops from the apple tree so his mother could make applesauce that weekend. The day was cool and gray, and he had to work briskly to stay warm in his old sweatshirt. His hands were cold and stiff. He was so busy complaining to himself about how domestic his mother had become up here in the country that he only gradually became aware of a rhythmic *creak, creak, creak* coming from the schoolyard. When he glanced over, he saw Claire swinging on the swings. She was alone, and she was watching him with the same inscrutable intensity that she always did, and that made Riley squirm.

His first thought was that she must be freezing. She was wearing the same thin dress he had seen her in at the close of school. No jacket. No sweater. He waved hesitantly, really no more than a brush through the air as if he had discovered a cobweb in front of his face. She waved back, a small wave, while she held tight to the swing with the other hand. Riley nodded and went back to raking up the drops. The gnarled old tree had not been tended properly in years, and the apples showed this want of care. They looked like misshapen lumps of yellow and red clay, pitted with black spots, and, as Riley looked at them more closely, maybe even wormholes. They don't look like anything I want to eat, he thought, not even if they were drowned in cinnamon.

When he looked back fifteen minutes later, Claire was still swinging and still watching him. Finally, he put the rake down and walked over.

"Hi," he said. "Aren't you cold?"

"No," she replied. She kept her legs pumping, back and forth, back and forth while the swing traced a small crescent in the air.

"Would you like my sweatshirt?" he pressed.

"No," she said simply.

"Would you like me to push you?" he asked, feeling a need to offer something that she might accept.

Her eyes grew big. "Oh, yes," she said eagerly. "I love pushes. Mawy pushes me up over hew head."

Well, I still don't know who Mawy is, but if Mawy can push you over her head, so can I, he thought. He paused to look at Claire. She was so thin. She couldn't weigh more than fifty pounds.

He walked behind the swing, and when Claire came up toward him he grabbed the seat and pushed for all he was worth. The swing went down so low he almost stumbled, but then it rose in front of him, and as he pushed it, it climbed higher and higher, taking on a life of its own, until he was running out beneath it and could hear the whoosh of air as it started back. Even before he turned to admire his work, he could hear Claire shrieking with delight, and the noise startled him. He had not known she was capable of loudness, of such a demonstration of joy. It was enough to keep him going for a good fifteen minutes as he raced from the front of the swing's arc to the rear and grabbed the swing seat and started over again. To his surprise, or maybe because his arms were growing numb, Claire grew lighter and lighter. Not once did she stop laughing, egging him on.

"There you are."

Riley heard the calm voice before he figured out what direction it was coming from. And then he saw her. She was from his class in school. Riley tried to remember her name, but after weeks of consciously not paying attention, it took a moment to come to him: Mary. That was her name: Mary St. Francis. He had noticed her because she was the only other member of the seventh grade who seemed to care anything about school. She was tall and solidly built, with broad shoulders, deep dark eyes, and black hair that reached almost to her waist. She was pretty, in an Indian kind of way, Riley thought, and she was quiet in class, like he was, but she was as alert as a deer, and she knew every answer to every question. Suddenly, he could see the similarities between Claire and Mary. Mawy was Mary. He had known her all along.

Riley caught the swing as it swung back into his hands and chased after it to slow it down until it stopped and Claire hopped off.

"I've been looking for you," Mary said to her sister. "You shouldn't leave without telling me where you're going. Daddy is mad. I'm supposed to be home starting supper."

"I was swinging," Claire said innocently, as if that explained everything.

"I'm sorry. I guess it's my fault," Riley said, feeling guilty for having kept her. Perhaps if she hadn't been having such a good time, she would have gone home.

"It's not your fault," Mary said, addressing him for the first time and smiling shyly. "I could hear her laughing clear across the green."

"It was so much fun!" Claire said. "Wiley can push even highew than you can!"

"I've been wondering who Wiley was." Mary laughed. "I should have guessed."

"And I should have guessed who Mawy was." Riley laughed, too.

They both turned toward the sound of a car with a broken muffler approaching. A white sedan was wheezing its way up the street beside the green to the school. It died in front of them in a cloud of smoke, and a large dark-haired man climbed awkwardly out, pushing his feet into the air as if he were trying to clear hurdles and not just the low rise of the door frame.

"Get over here," the big man ordered gruffly. His words, few as they were, ran together.

No one moved.

"Hi, Daddy," Mary said quietly.

Riley felt the hair on the back of his neck prickle.

"I left a note for you telling you to start supper," Mr. St. Francis snarled. "That there was an order, and I expect you to do it, no questions asked. Then I go home and find that Claire has run off and now you're gone, too, and there ain't no dinner on the stove."

"Claire didn't run off," Mary said.

Riley turned and stared at her. Hadn't she just said that that was exactly what Claire had done?

"I sent her to Riley's to get some apples, and then I was afraid maybe she couldn't carry them, so I came after her. It's my fault."

"Your mom's got one of her sick headaches, and you take off with Claire like life ain't nothin' but fun and games. You know I got things to do." He waved a hand unsteadily, taking in the surroundings. "Somebody's gotta keep an eye on things. You don't see nobody else doin' it, do ya?"

"No, Daddy. I don't think there's anybody who can keep an eye on things the way you do," Mary said. "You go on and do what you have to do. We'll go right home."

She turned toward Claire and offered her hand. Claire came to Mary's hand as if she were made of iron and the hand were a magnet. Then she stood just behind Mary, as if she had found a foxhole.

"I should take you both across my knee," Mr. St. Francis mumbled. "You ain't too big, you know."

"No, Daddy, I know. We'll just get those apples and go right home and get supper started, won't we, Claire?"

"Yes, Poppy," Claire said in a small voice.

"I'll—I'll get them for you. I was just going to do that," Riley offered. He turned and ran toward his house for a paper bag. When he came back outside, Mr. St. Francis was gone, but pale blue smoke and the smell of gasoline hung in the air. Mary and Claire had taken the few steps from the schoolyard into the Griffins' front yard, where the deformed apples he had been raking up lay in a lopsided pile.

"Thank you," Mary said. "But you don't have to give us any apples. By the time I put supper on the table, he won't even remember them."

"Please take them," Riley said, sorrier than ever that they were such a pathetic excuse for apples. He leaned over and began grabbing handfuls of fruit to put in the paper bag. When the bag was bulging, he stood up and offered it to Mary, suddenly afraid that he had overfilled it. He had no idea how far she had to walk with it.

"Really," she repeated. "It's okay. He'll never know."

"I want you to have them," he insisted.

"What do you say, Claire?" Mary turned to her sister.

"Thanks, Wiley. And thank you fow the swings, too," Claire said.

"Anytime," Riley said, and meant it.

✄ ✄ ✄

Sam "What's-his-name," which is how Riley thought of him, came to dinner that night and fell through the porch steps. Riley was in the cavernous dining room, with its faded, flowery wallpaper and his grandparents' sideboard as big as a rowboat. He was putting knives, forks, and spoons around the small round table that sat at its center when he heard a loud splintering of wood and then a crash. When he and his mother reached the porch, Sam was gingerly pulling his long legs out of a hole in the steps.

"Sam! Are you all right?" Riley's mother asked anxiously.

She reached down and offered a hand to pull him out. Sam looked unsure about whether to test the next step with his weight. In the end, he half crawled and half walked up the last few steps, scuttling like a crab, Riley thought, until he had found wood on the porch that he determined was sound enough to support his weight. Not that he weighed very much, Riley noted again. Sam looked like the scarecrow from *The Wizard of Oz*.

"I don't think there will be any loss of life," Sam joked, but he limped into the house and checked himself over in the light of the kitchen. A small red stain was spreading down his right pant leg. He pulled the cloth up gingerly and revealed a long, oozing scrape on his shin.

"Riley, go upstairs and get the first-aid cream and the bandages," his mother ordered.

"No, really, I'm okay," Sam protested futilely.

"Even though it was only as a receptionist," Riley's mother said, "I worked in a doctor's office for too many years. While I keep getting dinner ready, Riley's going to wash that cut and put a Band-Aid on it."

When Riley returned to the kitchen, his mother had a bowl of soapy warm water ready and waiting.

Carefully, Sam pulled his pant leg up again to expose the scrape. The first thing Riley noticed were the scars— lots of pockmarks, a few scars as fat as his finger, and one angry-looking scar that must have been six inches long, still purple and shiny though it was obviously years old.

"Is that from shrapnel?" Riley asked in wonder. He froze with his hand and the washcloth in the air.

"Riley!" His mother spoke sharply. "That's rude!"

"No. It's from being careless. I fell through a rotted roof and broke my leg when I hit the floor," Sam said in a way that quietly but firmly closed the door on the subject.

Embarrassed, Riley lowered his head and dipped the washcloth in the soapy water and then dabbed at the cut. Every time he dabbed, Sam flinched. What a baby—for someone who had been to Vietnam, Riley thought meanly. He must have seen lots worse over there. You'd think he could stand a little soap.

He had no sooner finished his Florence Nightingale routine than Sam pulled his pant leg down and put him to work.

"Riley, would you mind going back out to see if you can find the bag I was carrying?" Sam asked. "Be careful, that third step's a killer."

Ha, ha. When did I become an errand boy? Riley complained silently as he went across the dark porch to the edge of the steps. He walked cautiously, certain that at any moment the floor would open up and swallow him, too. A brown bag lay on the top step, wet and darkly stained in the twilight. He picked it up with two fingers, and carrying it in front of him as if it were a lunch someone had stepped on in the cafeteria, he went back into the kitchen.

Mrs. Griffin looked up.

"Riley! What is that?" she gasped. "Is that blood?"

Sam laughed a laugh of real amusement, a brief burst of sound that exploded in the kitchen. "Those are tomatoes from my garden. Or they were. I'll bet if Riley looks, though, the zucchini survived. Nobody can kill a zucchini."

Later, they were all glad he had brought it, even Riley, who usually hated zucchini, because when his mother pulled the chicken from the oven—the chicken he had been looking forward to because it smelled so good while it roasted—Sam took a deep breath and sighed. "Kate, I should have thought to say something beforehand."

Riley's mother looked up from tossing the salad and waited.

"It smells delicious. But I don't eat meat," he said. "I haven't for a long time."

"Oh!" she said, obviously taken aback.

"I suppose I should have asked," she said, the color rising in her cheeks. "We'll just put the chicken aside. Riley and I can eat it tomorrow."

"No, please," Sam insisted. "You go ahead and eat it now. I'll eat around it."

"Nonsense," Riley's mother said firmly. Riley knew that Sam would never win this one. "I can do better than that."

Wait! Riley wanted to shout. I eat meat! I love roast chicken! It's my favorite! I'll eat the whole thing!

But his mother was already putting rice on to cook.

"Give me twenty minutes," she said.

That was how they came to sit down to dinner, not to roast chicken, which Riley could almost taste because he wanted it so badly, but to some casserole his mother had invented at the last minute, filled with shredded zucchini, rice, onion, corn, and cheese.

It's not what I'd choose for my birthday dinner, Riley

thought as he ate, but he was hungry enough by the time it landed on the table that whatever it was was better than starvation.

"I'm very sorry about the steps," Riley's mother said over apple pie, for what Riley thought must have been the tenth time. "I told you. The place is a wreck. Absolutely everything needs attention. I've bought lots of paint, but that's only a Band-Aid to hide the bigger problems until I can afford to fix them properly."

"You need some help, Kate," Sam said, bending over to rub his shin and looking around at the peeling wallpaper, torn in places from the strain of holding up the sagging plaster wall behind it. "I'm working on two jobs right now, but I've got time evenings and weekends. I can help you out."

"I have to watch my money right now, Sam, until I find a job," Riley's mother said. "But thank you very much for the offer."

"Don't worry about the money," Sam said. "Like I said, no wife, no children. I've got plenty of free time and I make enough to get by. In the meantime, I suggest you use the front door."

He turned to Riley. "Riley can help me," Sam said. "He was great working on the window. He can be an apprentice."

Riley's hand froze with a bite of apple pie halfway to his mouth and vanilla ice cream dripping onto his plate.

Wait a minute! he thought. He was sorry, of course, that Sam had gotten hurt, but Riley's plan was that the old house would fall down around their ears. He and his mother couldn't do much more than change a light bulb. Falling through the back steps had been an act of genius. If Riley had known they were that rotten, he would have jumped on them himself earlier. He looked at his mother hard, trying to send her frantic signals so she would tell Sam that they appreciated the offer but would manage on their own. He certainly wasn't going to help! But Mrs. Griffin and Sam were already on their feet clearing the table. They weren't paying any attention to him at all.

❧ *Chapter* FOUR

When Riley arrived home from school on Monday afternoon, his mother announced that she had found a job working as receptionist for the pediatrician in town while the doctor's regular receptionist took time off to have a baby.

Sam arrived the next Friday evening with more zucchini and tomatoes and his tool belt.

In no time at all, it seemed to Riley, Sam was coming two and three nights a week, and they were all eating brown rice, shredded potato pancakes, and carrot salad with raisins and honey. But Sam worked. Riley had to say that for him. He fixed the porch steps, filling Sharon's quiet evenings two nights running with the whine of a power saw and the steady staccato of hammering. Then he fixed the toilets so they wouldn't drip all the time and replaced some of the old pipes with ones that didn't rattle and groan every time someone used water somewhere in the house. He took the upstairs bathroom door off its hinges and sanded it down so it would fit in its frame, which had shifted as the house had settled over its long life. He put up some shelves in Riley's room so that

Riley could unpack the boxes he had shoved in his closet—if he ever chose to settle in, his mother said.

Between Sam's visits, he always left a little list of chores for Riley and his mother: sand the front door, paint the woodwork in the kitchen, pull the nails out of the old storm windows. Maybe this is what apprentices do, Riley thought, but it feels more like slavery.

"I don't see why I have to do all this work," Riley complained one evening as he worked beside his mother in the kitchen. She was using her hair dryer to melt the glue that was barely holding the ancient linoleum in place. As the linoleum lost its grip on the wood floor below, his job was to tug at it until it broke off in brittle pieces. Then he threw the pieces into a growing pile. In his opinion, what he and his mother were doing just made the whole place look worse. But no one asked for his opinion.

"You're not doing it all," his mother pointed out. "I'm helping."

"Well, then 'we.' I don't understand why *we* have to do all this work."

His mother turned off the hair dryer and sat back on her haunches.

"You don't see anybody else around, do you?" she asked. She wiped the back of her hand across her forehead and directed a strand of hair behind her ear. "Don't be ungrateful, Riley. Sam is doing all of this for nothing.

We could never afford to have anyone do this for us," she reminded him.

But to Riley, Sam's hammering sounded like someone putting nails in a coffin. He didn't want the house to look better. He didn't want his mother to like the place any more than she already did. He was discovering that each night of lentils seemed to inspire Sam and his mother to cook up more home-improvement projects. It was beginning to look more and more unlikely that he would ever leave Sharon.

The only time Riley had peace was after school, when he came home to an empty house. Then he deliberately walked past the note his mother had left him on the counter with a few small tasks scrawled on it and went directly upstairs to his bedroom.

He was working on a paper chain, the kind he remembered making in kindergarten with strips of brightly colored paper rolled into links. He'd bought the paper at the store and hoped that no one would ask him what it was for. He needn't have worried. No one had taken much notice of him except to ask how his mother was. At home he cut the sheets into strips. Each link stood for one day in this miserable place. He had used tacks to pin the chain in a corner near the ceiling. It had been pretty pathetic at first, looking as insignificant as a spider's web, but then he had switched to using slightly bigger links. It worked. Now he could see the progress every day as the chain stretched closer to the floor. When it grew long enough, he intended to drape it like a swag from corner to corner.

"That's festive," Riley's mother had said as she saw it taking shape. "What are you celebrating?"

"Nothing," Riley said, and he meant it.

Next he did his homework. Usually it took him about ten minutes. The fractions and long division he was assigned he had already learned in the second half of sixth grade in his old school. In science, everyone was falling asleep while the teacher talked endlessly on about nutrition and good eating habits. He longed to tell them all what he was learning about meat deprivation, but he had sworn to himself never to volunteer an answer as long as he attended the Sharon Consolidated School, and the issue didn't seem big enough, even to him, to warrant changing this course of his life.

The problem after he finished his homework was, now what? He was tired of playing chess with himself. He had a few books on the subject, and sometimes he opened one of them and studied plays, but what was the point if he didn't have anyone to play with? He was actually glad that the days were getting colder, because he kept his window closed more often now. With the window closed, he didn't have to listen to Tim and his rowdy gang of ruffians hooting and hollering after school in the parking lot next door as they chased their hockey puck around like mad dogs trying to grab their tails. They had been carrying their sticks around at school for weeks, as if waiting for an ice rink to fall from the sky, but so far they were still batting around the puck on the school's asphalt and making too much noise, much too much noise. He could see them all four years from now, big goons with red-and-black varsity jackets roaming the halls and bullying all the weaker kids, himself included. Riley never gave a thought to joining them. After the disastrous opening day of school, the lines had been pretty well drawn, and Riley was on the side that tried to stay out of the way.

✕ ✕ ✕

Toward the end of October, on the Saturday before Halloween, Riley trudged up the green from the general store, the mail in his hand. From his house, he could hear the whine of a power tool. As he rounded the corner to the back porch, he found Sam on a ladder installing a basketball net above the garage.

"Morning, Riley," Sam said.

"I don't play basketball," Riley reminded him, not bothering to return the greeting of the man who was making it harder and harder for him and his mother to pack up and leave.

"I know," Sam said, climbing down off the ladder. "It's just a gift. I used to spend a lot of time alone when I was your age, and I must have shot a million baskets filling that time. It's there if you want it. The ball is in the garage." Sam went up the back steps he had replaced, crossed the porch floor he had reinforced, and went into the kitchen where, Riley had no doubt, he had more projects in mind for all of them.

"Jeez!" Riley said to the wind. "I tell him I'm never going to unpack the boxes in my room, and he builds me shelves. I tell him I don't play basketball, and he puts up a net for me. Maybe if I tell him I don't drive, he'll give me a car, and I can finally get out of this place."

All three of them spent the afternoon painting the living room the color of egg yolks.

"If it can't be repaired, it can at least be cheery," said Riley's mother, surveying the cracked and chipped plaster. In the past month, they had sold or given away much of the heavy, worn furniture that Riley's grandparents had owned. But this house was so much bigger than their old one that its rooms dwarfed the furniture that was left. While the paint dried, they struggled to move the furniture around to some congenial arrangement. When the last side table had found its place, Riley's mother went off to the kitchen to dig up some chocolate chip cookies and apple cider.

"Why don't you two take a break and do something for fun?" she suggested as she left the room.

Sam and Riley looked at each other like strangers.

"Basketball?" Sam asked.

"Chess," Riley said.

"Well, I don't know much about chess," Sam confessed, "but I'm willing to learn."

Riley brought his chess set down and proceeded to give Sam a lesson. The object, he told himself, was to give Sam enough information to make him an interesting opponent, but not so much that the scent of winning would make him want to play very often. The fewer ties between them, the better. All around them, the smell of fresh paint pinched their noses.

"The little ones, they're pawns," Riley explained, taking the first chess pieces from the storage box. He put one in its place to show Sam where to put his pieces. When that row was filled, Riley picked up a rook and put it in the corner.

"It looks like a castle, but it's called a rook. It can move any number of squares forward and backward and to the side, but not on the diagonal," he explained, watching Sam carefully to see if he was taking it all in.

To Riley's surprise, Sam picked up the general idea of the game and its pieces pretty quickly. Riley was fascinated watching him use his long prayer hands to move everything quietly into place. Everything he did, he did quietly, Riley thought to himself. For the first time, Riley was struck by Sam's eyes. They were more than just dark; they were deep and intelligent. They didn't miss anything, but they didn't give much away either. Riley had the feeling that there was someone else entirely behind those eyes.

Sam was playing with the white pieces, and Riley explained that the white player always makes the first move. Sam studied the board as if he knew what he was doing, and finally reached out and moved a pawn forward.

Riley quickly moved a black pawn into position.

"You're too fast." Sam laughed. "I need more time to think."

It won't help you, Riley thought.

Three moves later, Riley said, "Checkmate."

"How did you do that?" Sam asked incredulously.

"It's called the Blitzkrieg," Riley said. "It's an old play if you know what you're doing and your opponent doesn't."

"I guess you're right about that," Sam admitted. "Looks like I'm going to have to do some homework before I let you try to humiliate me again. Heck, that wasn't even long enough for a break. Let's shoot a few hoops."

Riley hesitated.

"Fair is fair," Sam said. "The least you can do is let me show you that I'm competent at something."

They donned jackets and went out into the gray afternoon to shoot baskets while their hands grew stiff and clawlike in the cold. Although he had never played any more basketball than he was compelled to in gym class, Riley had seen enough of it to know right away that Sam was pretty good. He bent his tall frame into his dribbles, and when he shot, he came off his feet like an uncoiled spring. He was as graceful in his moves as a cat, and he had a good eye for the basket.

When Riley's turn came, his face grew red with embarrassment even before he made his first move. When he dribbled, he had to look down at his hand to keep the ball coming up into his palm. When he went in for his layups, he could not watch his hands and keep an eye on the location of the basket at the same time, so he often drove in too far and had to try to angle his shots from underneath the backboard. Once the ball even rebounded off the bottom corner of the backboard and hit him in the head before he could duck, knocking his glasses to the blacktop.

"Occupational hazard," Sam said lightly, retrieving Riley's glasses and handing them to him.

But Riley felt like an ox playing with a gazelle. "Did you play on the school team?" he asked, curious in spite of himself.

"Yeah, I did. Even earned a varsity jacket the year we won the division championship," Sam said. "I still have it tucked away somewhere." He dribbled out from under the basket, and without even looking over his shoulder laid in a hook shot with his left hand.

"You have a varsity jacket?" Riley asked, unable to hide his surprise. He tried to reconcile the image of soft-spoken Sam in a varsity jacket with the image he had of Tim in the one he would someday be wearing.

"Why is that so funny?" Sam asked, smiling.

"I don't know, you don't seem—what's the word—pushy enough," Riley said.

"Well, I've never been very pushy," Sam admitted. "But every sport has elements of grace and skill. I guess I could just shoot." And with that he took his rebound and dribbled out to the edge of the driveway. Up he went and up went the ball, and it flew out of his hands as if it were a bird taking flight and then dropped through the basket without touching the rim.

"Did you play in college?" Riley asked.

"For the little time that I was in college before the United States government informed me that it had other plans for me, I went to an art school. It didn't have sports teams," Sam explained.

"If you were in college, why didn't you just stay there until you finished?" Riley asked.

"That's not the way the draft worked for the Vietnam War. When Uncle Sam called, you went," Sam said. "Unless there was some physical reason you couldn't. And I wasn't that lucky."

"What do you mean?" Riley asked. "Didn't you want to go? I mean even if it was scary, we were fighting a war."

Sam stopped dribbling and looked squarely at him.

"I tried everything in the world not to go, Riley, except going to Canada," he said.

"But why?" Riley asked, his confusion growing. "It was a war. You were defending your country. Why wouldn't you go?"

"I believed it was an immoral war, Riley," Sam said. "I thought it was wrong for us to be there."

"Well, what did you do?" Riley demanded. He couldn't imagine not doing what your country asked you to do. There wasn't anything more important than your country, for Pete's sake, except maybe God. And the verdict was still out on God.

"I tried to be a conscientious objector," Sam said.

"'What's that?"

"It's when someone objects to fighting and is able to convince the draft board that it would go against his principles to fight," Sam explained. "I tried, but I lost."

"I just don't see how, if your country needs protecting, you could not fight," Riley protested. It sounded un-American to him.

"When I lost, I had to go. I didn't have any choice," Sam continued. "I went through basic training and then I was sent to Vietnam."

"So," Riley said, "you ended up going anyway." This sounded better to Riley, to have to fight if your country asked you to even if you didn't feel like it. What if your country went to war and nobody wanted to fight? What would happen then? Nobody would be safe.

"I went, but I didn't stay," Sam said.

"How long were you there?" Riley asked, unable to get out of his mind the news pictures he'd seen of soldiers from the Vietnam War snaking in long columns through flooded rice paddies waiting for the Vietcong to open fire. Even if you weren't pushy, like Sam, it would take a lot of guts to do that.

"One month," Sam said. His face was dark and tight, as if he were angry, but his voice was so low it was almost lost in the air. Riley noticed that his eyes seemed moist, but then his own eyes were tearing in the cold.

"Did you ever shoot anybody?" Riley asked.

"No," Sam said. "I thought we had no business being there. I refused to carry a gun."

"That's it? You just gave up and came home? I didn't think they let soldiers do that," Riley said, growing more and more confused.

"They don't," Sam said. He pitched the ball out from his chest with both hands and bounced it so it came up perfectly into Riley's cold hands.

"Tell your mom I'll get some of her chocolate chip cookies some other time. I've got some things I have to do." Sam turned and strode to his truck. He pulled open the driver's door. It groaned and creaked as if the metal were being tortured.

"But wait!" Riley protested. He didn't have all the answers he wanted.

"See you later, kiddo," Sam said, closing the door and starting the engine. As the truck started down the long road beside the green, its engine made its usual timpani of drum-and-rattle sounds.

Riley's mother appeared instantly at the porch door.

"Where's Sam going?" she asked.

"He couldn't stay," Riley said. Not here or there.

✢ *Chapter* FIVE

Riley promptly forgot about the basketball hoop. He passed it every day coming around the corner of the house after school, but he never even looked at it.

Sam stayed away for about a week, which seemed to worry Riley's mother, but he showed up unexpectedly one evening in early November with the light fixture Mrs. Griffin had ordered to replace the broken one in the living room. She had paid more than she wanted to for the new fixture, but it had brass arms and etched globes like the one that had hung there for decades.

"I'll just hang this up," Sam said, "and then I'll take off."

"Nonsense," said Riley's mother. "Stay for dinner. We have plenty."

"No, really," Sam said.

Riley agreed with him. Except during this recent short break, Sam ate altogether too many dinners at their house, in Riley's opinion. He opposed it on many grounds. For one, Sam usually felt that he should contribute something, and something usually turned out to be vegetables from his garden, which lately went to brussels sprouts and squash that came in all sorts of outlandish shapes and sizes. Second, when Sam joined them, they couldn't have meat. Right now, Riley knew that if Sam stayed for dinner they wouldn't be able to have ground beef in their spaghetti sauce, and Riley liked meat in his spaghetti sauce. Third, Sam's work around the house had gotten completely out of control. There was still a lot of what his mother called cosmetic work to do—painting and rewallpapering—but most of the old house's cantankerous problems had been fixed. Even Riley had to admit that it felt somewhat inhabitable, and that ran in the face of his plans to leave. Fourth, his most recent conversation with Sam had left him with an odd feeling in his stomach.

"I don't want to intrude," Sam insisted. "But I'm going to have to turn the power off for fifteen minutes while I wire in the new fixture."

Fifteen minutes in the dark turned into twenty and then twenty-five as Sam struggled to hang the new fixture working only by flashlight. Apprenticing once again, Riley was assigned the job of standing there holding the new fixture until he thought his arms would fall off. His mother remained in the lighted kitchen, working on their dinner and occasionally calling down the long hallway, cajoling Sam to change his mind. By the time she was able to come into the living room to admire the dazzling effect, she had worn Sam down.

Over dinner, Riley's mother asked him what he was studying in school these days. "Are you done with nutrition?"

"Finally," Riley said.

"What's next?" she asked.

"Bodily functions," Riley said.

"Well, I guess we don't need to talk about those at dinner," Sam said, laughing.

"What are you doing in history?" Riley's mother asked. She took another bite of spaghetti and started the garlic bread around for the second time.

"American, some Vermont," Riley said. He took another bite and swallowed it. "I know most of it already, except the Vermont stuff. I have to memorize the Gettysburg Address."

"Why?" Sam asked.

"I have to give it in front of the class on November nineteenth. That's the day Lincoln delivered it. This year is the hundred and seventeenth anniversary. Nobody else was willing to do it. I don't think anyone else even knew what it was. Except Mary," he added. "She probably knows. Anyway, when nobody volunteered, Mr. Aja asked me if I'd do it. I said okay. It's no big deal. It isn't even very long."

"Four score and seven years ago," his mother said. "I don't know how much further I can go. *Our fathers brought forth on this continent, a new nation.* I think that's how it starts."

"Conceived in Liberty, and dedicated to the proposition that all men are created equal," Sam continued. *"Now we are engaged in a great civil war, testing whether that nation, or any nation so conceived and so dedicated, can long endure."*

Riley stopped chewing and looked at Sam.

"Why do you know it?" he asked.

"Because it's a beautiful speech full of noble thoughts. It explains why men sometimes have to fight," Sam explained. "Sometimes—but not always—fighting is the right thing to do."

"Would you please excuse me," Riley's mother said. She stood up, and in a few seconds Sam and Riley could hear her footsteps as she climbed the long flight of stairs to the second floor. She didn't come down for ten minutes. Riley and Sam finished their spaghetti without speaking, the only sound the ringing of their forks on their plates. When she finally did return, she was carrying a dirty white box a little bigger than a shoebox. She put it on the table and lifted off the lid.

"I'm sorry," she said. "It took me a while to find this. It's been packed away for so long, and then with the move and everything, I couldn't even remember which moving box I'd put it in."

She lifted out something wrapped in tissue paper about the size of a pair of slippers and handed it to Riley.

"Be careful," she warned him. "They're very fragile."

Riley carefully began to unwrap the tissue paper. When he was through, he had a badly scratched and worn pair of binoculars in his hand. At one time they had been black, and they still mostly were, but now the paint was pitted and dulled. A pair of thick brass stripes had been laid down around the rim of the larger lenses, and two other pairs of brass stripes encircled the canisters above and below where the stem for focusing joined them in the middle. At one time the brass must have been shiny, but now it was as dull and flat as the black paint. A light chocolate–colored webbed strap with a rusted buckle had been threaded through the center of the binoculars.

"What're these?" he asked his mother.

"Turn them over," his mother urged. "And look closely."

There, on the side, scratched in as if with the point of a nail and rusted over, was the name Silas Griffin.

"He was your great-great-great-grandfather," his mother explained. "He fought in the Civil War, and these were his binoculars. In fact, he fought at the Battle of Gettysburg. Your father wanted you to have them when you were older, and I had almost forgotten about them until you mentioned your speech. I'm sorry I don't know more about them. Maybe your father did, but he never said anything more to me. I do know that they were very precious to him, and that he wanted you to have them when you were old enough to appreciate them." Riley's mother's eyes had filled with tears. "Excuse me," she said again, and stood up and left the room. This time Riley and Sam did not hear her footsteps on the stairs, but in half a minute they heard the squeak of the tired couch springs in the living room as she sat down in the dark, without even bothering to turn on the new light.

Riley was shocked. He turned the binoculars over and rubbed his hand across them. Where the paint was pitted, it was coarse, like sandpaper. As he stretched out the strap, he thought it might be so brittle that it would break, but it was unexpectedly pliant and soft, so he hung the binoculars around his neck.

"That's pretty cool," Sam said. "I don't think I've ever seen anything like that."

Riley took off his glasses. Gently, he brought the eyepieces up and looked through the doorway into the lighted kitchen beyond. The old glass was thick and heavy and slightly clouded by ancient imperfections. The eyepieces were uncomfortably close together and little larger than a nickel. Obviously, the binoculars were old and he shouldn't expect them to be as good as modern ones. But they were surprisingly good. He adjusted the nosepiece until they rested more comfortably against his nose, and then fiddled with the one screw in the centerpiece. It moved grudgingly, but gradually the new sink and countertop in the kitchen came into focus and filled his view.

"How are they?" Sam asked.

"Not bad," Riley said in surprise. Without thinking, he added, "They're pretty neat. Here, try them." He carefully lifted the strap over his head and handed the binoculars across the table.

Sam turned toward the kitchen.

"That's amazing," he said, sounding as if he had a cold as he pressed the binoculars down upon his nose.

"I can't believe they were really at Gettysburg," Riley said. It seemed incredible to him that a gift of such value would fall almost out of heaven into his lap.

"Even more than that, they belonged to your great-great-great-grandfather. You might have a true hero in your past," Sam said. "You probably don't know this because you're a New York suburb kid, but Vermont played a big part in the Battle of Gettysburg. In fact, Vermonters helped carry the day at Pickett's Charge."

"What's that?" Riley asked.

"It was the Confederacy's last great stand," Sam explained. "Twelve thousand men tried to storm the Union line. Two thirds of them fell or were captured. The war lasted another two years, but the South never had another chance like that one to break the Union."

"Do you think those binoculars might have belonged to someone from Vermont?" Riley asked, amazed by the evening's turn of events.

"Who knows?" Sam said. "You know what I know, which is that your mother and father met at the University of Vermont, you're living in Vermont now, and the binoculars came down from Silas Griffin at Gettysburg to you."

Later, after Sam had gone home, while his mother was washing the dishes and Riley was drying them, he kept looking at the binoculars positioned as carefully as a museum display on the new countertop.

"You don't know anything more about them?" Riley asked his mother for the third time.

"I'm sorry, honey, I don't," she said patiently. "I always thought that your father would be the one to give the binoculars to you. I never asked him much about them. You know, Riley, I just thought he would be here. I never imagined that he wouldn't be."

"What about his family?" Riley asked.

"I don't know much about them either," she explained. "Your father was an only child, and when I met him in college, only your grandmother was still living. And she died within a year of when we were married. I never met another relative. At your father's and Cassie's funeral, we were the only family he had there. As far as I know, we were all he had left."

"But don't you know *anything*?" Riley demanded. "Where he grew up or anything? Didn't you ask him anything at all?"

"Your father grew up in a small town in southern New Jersey," his mother said. "He spent summers on an old farm in Vermont that belonged to his aunt and uncle—your grandfather's brother—and because of that he went to the University of Vermont to study engineering. We met in college. After we graduated, we moved to Stony Point because your father got a job there, and you were born two years later."

"Did the binoculars come from Grandpa's brother?" Riley asked.

"He would have been a Griffin, too," his mother agreed. "I guess that would be possible."

"So they *are* from Vermont," Riley announced.

"Perhaps," his mother conceded. "But I really don't know anything more than I've told you. It doesn't seem like enough to know about your father, does it?"

"No, it doesn't," Riley said sharply. He already knew most of what his mother had just told him, but the binoculars shocked him. They gave him the smallest piece of information about his father and then left him hanging like a book balanced on the edge of a table. The frustration was almost like real pain. If that was all his mother could tell him, there didn't seem to be any hope of connecting the pieces he knew.

Later, while he was propped up in bed reading, his mother came in and sat on the end of his bed. The binoculars were lying on a towel on the floor by the head of the bed. He didn't want to risk them falling over. Riley had also thought about hanging them by the strap from the bedpost, but he was afraid that might be too hard on the old webbing.

"Think how carefully those binoculars have been saved through the years, passed down from one generation to the next," his mother said. "That's a remarkable piece of history to have in your hands, Riley. Your father would have loved to have seen your interest in history develop. He would be very proud of you."

"Sam says Vermont played a big part in the Battle of Gettysburg," Riley said, temporarily putting aside his confusing feelings about Sam in order to relish the information Sam had given him. "He says everything might have been lost if the Vermonters hadn't saved the day at Pickett's Charge. Those binoculars might have belonged to a hero." He looked at the binoculars, still unable to believe that they were his.

"I vaguely remember that from studying Vermont history when I was going to school here. But that was a very long time ago." She laughed.

"The Battle of Gettysburg or your going to school here?" Riley teased.

"Both." She laughed again and stood up. "Sweet dreams." She kissed Riley on the only place where he still let himself be kissed, the top of his head, and then paused for a minute to admire the growing paper chain, now draped in a graceful swag from one corner of the room to another. "This will be ready just in time for Christmas. You will love Christmas here. It's beautiful. It's one of the things I remember best."

Chapter SIX

Riley stood in front of the class and looked into a sea of mostly dull eyes. From the back corner, where she always sat, Mary waited, her eyes fierce and alert but her face as flat and expressionless as the bottom of a skillet. He cleared his throat and pushed his glasses back into place.

"Four score and seven years ago," he began, his voice faltering in the face of such lack of interest, even though he had known it would be like this. What else could he expect from most of his classmates? But their indifference made him angry, and he plowed on, his voice getting stronger: *"our fathers brought forth on this continent, a new nation, conceived in Liberty, and dedicated to the proposition that all men are created equal.*

"Now we are engaged in a great civil war, testing whether that nation, or any nation so conceived and so dedicated, can long endure. We are met on a great battle-field of that war. We have come to dedicate a portion of that field, as a final resting place for those who here gave their lives that that nation might live. It is altogether fitting and proper that we should do this.

"But, in a larger sense, we can not dedicate—we can not consecrate—we can not hallow—this ground. The brave men, living and dead, who struggled here, have consecrated it, far above our poor power to add or detract. The world will little note, nor long remember what we say here, but it can never forget what they did here. It is for us the living, rather, to be dedicated here to the unfinished work which they who fought here have thus far so nobly advanced. It is rather for us to be here dedicated to the great task remaining before us—that from these honored dead we take increased devotion to that cause for which they gave the last full measure of devotion—that we here highly resolve that these dead shall not have died in vain—that this nation, under God, shall have a new birth of freedom—and that government of the people, by the people, for the people, shall not perish from the earth."

✄   ✄   ✄

Riley had barely begun when he saw Sam slip through the doorway at the back of the classroom. No one turned but Mr. Aja, who gave Sam a smile and a short nod. Sam nodded back and stood quietly, watching and listening, his work clothes hanging off him as if they belonged to a man twice his size. Riley stumbled briefly in surprise and almost lost his train of thought, but the language was as strong and powerful as a wave, and it carried him along.

The applause was halfhearted, at best, but Riley hadn't expected any at all. Sam, Mary, and Mr. Aja kept going for another second after the others stopped, and some members of the class turned to locate the source of the enthusiasm. Then an embarrassing silence fell over the room. Sam took that opportunity to leave as quietly as he had come.

At lunch recess, everyone went to their accustomed spots: younger children, including Claire, to the fenced-in playground with its slides and monkey bars; high schoolers to the front lawn, where they milled about, heckling and teasing each other good-naturedly and standing too close to one another; and the sixth, seventh, and eighth graders to wherever they could carve out space for themselves. For most of the boys this meant playing hockey on the basketball court, while the girls huddled in the lee of the building. The day was raw and sunless, a bitter day for Riley to stand around doing nothing, with his hands shoved deep in his pockets for warmth, so he headed away from the building toward the cemetery on the rise behind the school. Minutes later, walking back toward the school and praying that recess would soon be over, he was startled to hear one of the hockey players call out to him.

"That was pretty funny that Sam Mitchell would come to hear you give your big speech."

Riley turned his head. That goon Tim Ferris was walking toward him. Riley stopped: What Tim had said may have struck him as funny, but it hadn't sounded funny to Riley, at least not the way Tim had said it.

"Why was it funny?" asked Riley, who detected something in the boy's voice that put him on the defensive. He looked at Tim's big hands clutching his hockey stick, and he was angry with himself for feeling small. Tim's fists looked like they could break sticks as big around as Riley's wrists. Riley knew his fists looked like they moved chess pieces around a playing board. He took one step backward and immediately regretted it.

"The whole war thing," Tim sneered, coming even closer. "Wouldn't think Sam Mitchell would dare show up when anyone's talking about something that took any courage." He spit out the last word, as if it had gotten too close to Sam Mitchell's name and needed to get away fast.

"What?" Riley demanded.

"You don't know, do you?" Tim jeered, a note of surprise in his voice.

"I know more than you think I do," Riley said, hoping that it was true.

"Yeah, well, then you know that your loser friend Sam Mitchell was kicked out of the army. Turned tail and ran almost as soon as he landed in 'Nam," Tim said. "He's ashamed, and he oughta be. That's why he lives like a hermit up in the woods—or at least he did until you and your mom showed up."

Riley felt as if he'd been stung. He was grateful for the bracing air. It took the color out of everyone's cheeks, so his shocked white ones didn't look out of the ordinary.

Tim laughed, a cruel, cold sound that hung in the air like an icicle; then he took off, chasing the puck and muscling everyone out of the way.

Riley stood rooted to the spot until the bell rang. He filed back into the warm classroom with the others and took his seat in math, but he wasn't paying attention.

"Riley, Riley Griffin?" Mr. Temple asked sharply. "Pay attention, unless you're sick. Are you sick?"

"No, sir," he said. "I'm okay." But that wasn't how it felt.

Later he was kneeling, taking his books from his locker at the end of the school day, when a hand appeared in front of his nose with a note in it. He looked up.

"I have to go home right away or my dad will give me hell. You did a good job today," Mary said. She held the note steadily in front of him until he was forced to focus on it and take it. Then she disappeared into the milling crowd.

Ten minutes later, at home and up in his bedroom, he sat on the bed and unfolded the note.

"Don't listen to them. Sam Mitchell is a good person," was all it said.

"Where's Sam?" Riley asked after dinner while he and his mother were painting doors. It was another task on Sam's endless list of chores. Riley was tired of apprenticing. He hadn't asked to do any of this in the first place, and he was royally sick of all the work.

"He's trying to finish up a job," she explained. "He said he probably wouldn't be by all week."

Hallelujah, Riley thought.

"He showed up at school today," Riley said.

"Why?" his mother asked in surprise.

"He came to hear me recite the Gettysburg Address," Riley said.

"He did?" Her voice rose higher.

"He snuck in the back of the class just after I started and listened. He left as soon as it was over," Riley said.

"Well, that was very nice of him, although it must have been a surprise to you," his mother said.

"I wasn't the only one who was surprised," Riley said.

"What do you mean by that?" she asked.

Riley didn't say anything.

"Riley, what are you talking about? Who else was surprised?" She put down her paintbrush and studied him.

"Some of the boys were talking about him," Riley said.

"What did they say?" his mother asked.

He took a deep breath.

"One of them said he was kicked out of the army," Riley said. "He said Sam went to Vietnam and wouldn't fight. He said the army sent Sam home for being a coward. He said Sam doesn't have any friends in town but us, that we're the only ones who will have anything to do with him."

"Some of that is true," his mother said after considering it. "I know you and Sam have talked about this a bit. What did he say?"

"He told me he thought the Vietnam War was wrong and he couldn't fight. So he came home," Riley said.

"Well, that's right as far as it goes, but it's not the whole story. Sam was thrown in jail for refusing to fight, and when they realized that he was not going to change his mind, they gave him a dishonorable discharge and sent him home."

"So it's true he was afraid to fight," Riley said.

"I don't think he was any more afraid than anyone else was. He just thought the war was wrong. Many people did," his mother continued. "Your father and I protested against the Vietnam War. We marched against the war and carried candles in vigils while we were in college."

"But Dad—*he* would have gone if he'd been drafted," Riley insisted, hoping he was right about a man he barely remembered. "And he would have fought if that's what his country wanted. He wouldn't have let other men die for him."

"Maybe." His mother paused. "I don't know. But he was very lucky. He didn't have to make that choice. The draft at that time was run on a lottery. Every man, when he turned eighteen, received a lottery number based on the date of his birthday. Sam was unlucky enough to get a low number, and he was drafted out of college. Your father had a very high number, and he was never called. I remember the day the numbers were posted on the wall outside the dining hall at college. Some of the guys were sobbing because they knew they would have to leave and go off to fight and might never come back. Other guys were crying with relief because they knew they were safe. It was an awful time."

"Why couldn't Sam just do it?" Riley asked. "Everybody else did."

"Not everybody did, Riley. Sam was not alone. He was just the only one in Sharon. The Vietnam War was not like World War I and World War II, when people understood what they were fighting for. Sam didn't believe in destroying another country when he couldn't understand what might be gained for our country or for the world."

"What did people say?" he asked.

"According to your Mrs. Benedict, they said a lot," his mother said. "Some people thought he was a coward, and they still won't talk to him. A few—really, just a couple—thought he was a hero. Most people didn't know what to think, just like they didn't know what to think about the war itself."

"What did Sam say?" Riley asked.

"Nothing," his mother said. She plunged her paintbrush back into the paint. "He wouldn't talk about it with anyone. He still won't, although he has told both you and me a little of his story. When he came home, he built himself a cabin in the woods and he hardly left it for the next five years. Then he took up carpentry. He keeps pretty much to himself. You know most of the rest of it."

"No, I don't," Riley protested. "I think he should have stood up and fought, like he was supposed to. I think he was just afraid. I think maybe he was a coward."

"You will have to figure that out for yourself," his mother said softly, turning to look at him. "But I hope that when you finally learn enough about Sam to make up your own mind you will judge him fairly."

ꙮ *Chapter* SEVEN

Snow fell two days before Thanksgiving and the furnace died the same day. Riley came home from school shivering in his lightweight New York jacket, the one whose drab brown reminded him of the color the hills were turning as all the trees but the oaks dropped their last leaves. He knew as soon as he opened the back door that something was wrong. The air was frigid, almost as cold inside as outside. The basil that his mother had carefully dug up from a friendly neighbor's garden and potted to bring inside was withered in its pot above the kitchen sink. Riley looked around to see if any windows were broken or open, but when he couldn't find any, he called his mother at the doctor's office.

"Mom, I think the furnace is broken or something," he said. His teeth were chattering. "The house is freezing. Maybe we're out of oil."

"That can't be," his mother assured him. "I just had oil delivered last week." She sounded tired and discouraged. "It must be the furnace. But I can't leave here right now. The waiting room is full. Maybe you could call Sam. I think he said he'd be working in his workshop today."

So Riley called Sam. He had not spoken to Sam in a week, since November 19, the anniversary of the Gettysburg Address, and now he listened carefully when Sam answered the phone on the third ring. He listened for what he did not know, but Sam sounded quiet and calm, the way he always did.

"Sam, it's Riley," he said. "Mom told me to call you." He tried to say it so Sam would know that something had changed, so Sam would know that he had not called on his own.

"What's up?" Sam asked. If he was surprised to receive this first phone call from Riley, he did not let on. Neither did he show in any way that he objected to or was hurt by Riley's tone of voice.

"I'll come by in a little while, as soon as I finish up here," Sam said after Riley had explained the trouble. "I'm sure the house is cold, but it's not so cold outside that you have to worry about pipes freezing and breaking. At least, not right away. You find someplace warm to go for a few hours. I'll let myself in."

"Yeah, right—like there's any place to go," Riley mocked after he hung up. He dug the book he was reading out of his knapsack and lay down on the couch in the living room. But it was too cold. He reached for his grandmother's pink, orange, and yellow afghan, the one that made him think all the paint pots must have spilled in the kindergarten class, and spread it over his legs as he stretched out on the couch. He pulled it clear up to his chin, but he was still shivering. Then he began thinking that he might not want to be there when Sam arrived.

Skeptical that he could find anywhere in this one-store town to hide, he zipped his jacket up and headed out. He tried the library first, a ridiculous brick dinosaur with a pair of more ridiculous granite columns flanking the door, but it wasn't open. No surprise, he thought. His mother had taken him there soon after they arrived in Sharon, but after he had looked around at the worn carpet and the dozen shelves of books, comparing it to the new two-story library he had left behind in Stony Point, he had thought it was such a sorry excuse for a library that it was a joke. At the time, he hadn't been able to imagine ever being so desperate that he'd be driven here. Now he stood on the stoop and read the hours: Monday, Wednesday, Friday: 1–5 P.M.; Saturday mornings, 10–12. Maybe, just maybe, he thought, that information might come in useful sometime, but he didn't think so, and right now it didn't help him at all.

His shivering grew worse, and finally he crossed the street and went into the store.

"Can I help you, Riley?" Mr. Benedict asked. He was crouching in the middle of one of the aisles at the center of a half circle of big, opened cardboard boxes.

"No, thank you," Riley said. "The heat's off at our house and I'm freezing."

"Does your mom know?" Mr. Benedict asked.

"I called her," Riley said.

"Stay as long as you like," Mr. Benedict said, and he went back to stocking boxes of crackers.

That turned out to be not very long. Riley noted that the toy selection was unchanged since late summer. The same jacks and cards and Frisbees. Like anyone would be out trying to play Frisbee today, Riley thought.

The next minute, the bell on the front door tinkled.

"Got a deer," a deep male voice said.

"I'll be right with you," Mr. Benedict said.

Curiosity drew Riley to the front of the store. Mr. Benedict was taking off his apron and putting on a red plaid hunting jacket.

"Where's the deer?" Riley asked.

"Out in Walter Douglas's truck," Mr. Benedict said. He pointed to a certificate on the wall behind the cash register. "We're a deer weighing station. We sell them the license to hunt and then we record what they bring back. Of course, for some of them, the license is all they ever get." He smiled and shrugged as if he couldn't see the point of it all.

Riley followed Mr. Benedict outside to where the truck was parked. The deer was sprawled on its side in the bed. It had been gutted, and the cavity in its chest where its heart had once beat was empty except for the white ribs, whose tips were lined up as evenly as teeth.

The deer's ears still stood erect, as if on alert, but the danger was past. The deer's tongue lolled from its mouth, and its eyes were as lifeless as brown marbles.

The record taking took only a few minutes. Mr. Douglas and his hunting buddies hauled the deer from the back of the truck and laid it on a big scale that stood at the corner of the building while Mr. Benedict clipped a tag to one of the deer's ears. Then they counted the points on the antlers and measured their span. When the deer was back in the truck bed, the men stood around for a few more minutes talking with Mr. Douglas, admiring the fine rack on the deer's head and teasing him about the larger buck the hunters had seen but missed early that morning.

While they were all huddled around the bed of the truck, Mr. St. Francis pulled up in front of the store in his white ocean liner of a car with its deafening muffler. He opened the door of his car and pulled himself to a standing position.

"Whatcha' got there?" he asked as he wove a path over to the group.

"Walt got himself a deer," Mr. Benedict explained. The men all shuffled their positions and gave Mr. St. Francis plenty of room. Riley stepped back, off the store steps and into the shadows. Mr. St. Francis put his hand on the deer's neck.

"Yep, it's getting cold. Must be dead," Mr. St. Francis

said, as if there could be any doubt about a deer that didn't have its insides anymore. "I oughtta know. I've seen plenty of death in my time."

"You surely have," Mr. Benedict agreed gently, while the other men nodded. "What have you been up to, Stan?"

"Just keeping an eye on things," Mr. St. Francis said, as if everyone would understand.

"Why don't you go on home," Mr. Benedict suggested. "And here . . ." He disappeared into the store and came out half a minute later carrying a gallon of milk, which he handed to Mr. St. Francis.

Mr. St. Francis accepted the milk with a nod, and without offering to pay for it, he wove another path back to his car. They all listened to the car rumble and roar into the purple that fell just before darkness.

The men stood awkwardly in the silence that followed.

"There but for the grace of God," Mr. Benedict said, and turned to go back into his store.

The men clambered into the truck and pulled out with the head of Walter Douglas's buck still draped over the end of the tailgate. Riley watched as the lights from the store caught the deer's lifeless eyes and made them glow like green candles.

Twilight had fallen hard. Up the hill, Riley could see lights on in the downstairs windows of his house. It was too early for his mother to be home, so the lights must mean that Sam had arrived, Riley thought. That meant he still couldn't go home. He noticed that lights were also burning in his history classroom at the school. Without knowing exactly what he meant to do, he climbed the slight hill across the green and went in the front door of his school. He couldn't see anybody, but the dark door-ways of empty classrooms stretched before him like black keys on the piano.

Down the hall, he heard voices. When he followed them, he was shocked to find Mary and Mr. Aja playing chess. They were sitting on opposite sides of a classroom desk, and there were only a half dozen chess pieces left on the board. Mr. Aja was winning, and Mary was laughing, a sound Riley had never heard, as her teacher took his final few moves and swept in for his victory.

"Come in, come in, Mr. Griffin," Mr. Aja said warmly when he looked up and saw Riley standing at the door. Mr. Aja was older than most of the teachers at the school. Riley had heard he wasn't married, and that made him different, too. He was losing his dark hair, and he carried his reading glasses on a string around his neck, but with or without the glasses, he didn't miss a thing. Everyone in the seventh grade loved him. He had a tendency to call his students by their last names. "This is indeed a pleas-ant surprise. Do you play chess?"

As if anticipating Riley's answer, he stood up to offer Riley his chair.

"A little," Riley said. He hadn't really had enough time to judge the level of play, and he didn't want to overstate his skill. Better to be better than they think than not as good as they think, he decided.

"Good," Mr. Aja announced, apparently well satisfied with Riley's answer. "Play Miss St. Francis one more game. Mary St. Francis is the entire Sharon Consolidated School Chess Club. I will sit here and grade some papers until there is no place left for us to go but home." As he said this, he looked at Mary and winked.

Riley sat down awkwardly opposite Mary, and without a word he and Mary set up their pieces.

"That's promising, Miss St. Francis," Mr. Aja remarked, looking up from his desk and the pile of papers stacked there. His eyes twinkled with mischief. "He knows where the pieces go."

Mary opened. Pawn for pawn, pawn for pawn. Knight for knight. Bishop for bishop. Riley realized that he would not be able to impress her with the Blitzkrieg, because she clearly knew that strategy and was defending against it. They played for almost forty-five minutes without exchanging a word. Rooks, queens, knights, the last bishops, pawns. Almost everything fell. Finally, play was reduced to white king and white rook against black king. In three moves, Mary maneuvered Riley's king into the corner. Riley slowly laid his king on its side, the sign of capitulation.

"Good game," Mary said. She looked at him and smiled slightly. Her dark eyes were no less fierce, but her face was softer, not filled with the same determination to be educated that made her almost fearsome in class.

"You, too," Riley said and then felt foolish. She had obviously played a good game because she had beaten him.

Mr. Aja shuffled the papers on his desk.

"Well, do you want to join the team?" he asked good-naturedly. "You will swell our ranks. You will increase exponentially our chances of winning."

Riley hesitated, torn between continuing defiance against belonging to anything in Sharon and the warmth of their company.

"You don't have to decide now," Mr. Aja assured him. "Come by any Tuesday after school. That's when Miss St. Francis and I go at each other. We can take turns."

They put on their jackets.

"Can I give you a ride home, Mary?" Mr. Aja asked. His voice sounded different from the way it did in class, more personal and warm. "It's getting brisk out there."

"No, thanks, I'll be fine," Mary said quietly.

"Are you sure?" he asked.

"Yes, but thank you," she said. "It's the fourth Tuesday of the month, so my father is at the American Legion tonight. Claire and I will just go to bed before he gets home."

Riley noticed that she put on a jacket that was even thinner than his before she disappeared down the hallway. They heard the big metal front door clang shut behind her.

"You live just next door, don't you, Riley?" Mr. Aja asked as he flipped off the lights in the classroom.

"Yes, sir," Riley said. They walked together down the hallway in a school absolutely silent except for the sound of their footsteps echoing against cinderblock.

"I imagine Sharon seems like a lost star at the edge of the universe after the suburbs of New York City," Mr. Aja said as they closed and locked the front door. "I felt the same way ten years ago when I landed here from Chicago. But I discovered there is much to appreciate here. I don't see much evidence at school that you've made many—or indeed any—friends since you arrived, but not everyone is like the hockey-playing thugs at lunchtime. A few of your schoolmates could give you a run for your money. Mary and you have more in common than you know. Give it a chance."

Riley watched him walk to his car, get in, and turn on the engine. The headlights came on and swept across the green like a shooting star as Mr. Aja turned and headed for the main road. Riley glanced toward his house. There were lights on now on both floors, which probably meant that his mother was home. Light even peeked out from the single window in the basement, the only break in the massive granite blocks that held up the house.

Riley walked home and discovered a van sitting in the driveway with AL'S HEATING SERVICE printed on the side, its back doors flung open to the night as if a bomb had gone off inside it.

The house was still freezing.

A man who Riley could only guess was Al was trudging up from the cellar, a tool belt around his waist. He had a dark smudge across one cheek and his hands were black. Riley's mother was right behind him.

"You're going to have to replace it," Al was saying. "That's an elephant. Didn't even start out as an oil furnace. Somebody converted it from wood, twenty, maybe thirty years ago. I'm sorry, Mrs. Griffin, but you don't have any choice here. I can make it limp along through the night, but that's all. I'll be up bright and early tomorrow morning to put in a new one."

Riley's mother's face was pale and pinched. Riley had no idea what a new furnace cost, but this old house was big and hard to heat. A new furnace was bound to cost a lot of money. He decided he wouldn't mention tonight that his Stony Point winter jacket didn't seem to be worth much in Vermont winters—and it wasn't even officially winter yet. Sam came down the hall from the living room, an extension cord in his hand.

"I hooked up the space heater," he said, without acknowledging Riley. "If he can coax a little heat out of the furnace, I think it and the space heater together will keep your pipes from freezing tonight. But you're not going to want to sleep here."

"But I have to," Riley's mother protested. "I wouldn't dare leave a space heater running all night unattended. I could burn the whole house down."

"I know that," Sam said. "I'll sleep here, down in the living room, near the space heater. I can keep an eye on things. You and Riley go on over to my place. You'll be warm. It's unlocked. Just throw a few logs into the wood-stove, and you'll be fine. By tomorrow night, everything will be fixed and you can come back in time to make me a Thanksgiving dinner." He smiled at Riley's mother and then turned to Riley.

"You okay about spending a night in the woods?" he asked.

"I think I can handle that," Riley said, offended that Sam thought he was such a city kid that he might be afraid of the woods.

"Good, go get your things. And don't let the bears get your mother."

꙰   ꙰   ꙰

In a few minutes, Riley and his mother were in the car heading out of town.

"It's sweet of Sam to rescue us like this," she said.

What rescue? Riley thought. How much courage does it take to sleep in a cold house?

Riley had never been to Sam's cabin. His mother made one wrong turn in the dark before she found the right dirt road and headed up a hill into the woods. The leaves had fallen weeks ago, and the ancient maples lining the road stood silent as sentries, the branches of their massive crowns intertwined like hands in prayer above the dirt and gravel.

"You've never been here," his mother said, expressing more of a question than a statement.

"No," said Riley. "When were you here?"

"A month or two ago," she said. "I can't remember why you weren't with me. I asked to see his cabin, and he brought me."

"Why does he live way out here?" Riley demanded. He swept his arm in a small arc that took in everything: the uneven road, the bare ground beneath the canopy of naked treetops, the absence of everything else. "This is the middle of nowhere!"

"When he came back, most of the residents of Sharon did not embrace him," she explained, driving carefully up the rutted road. "He was more comfortable living off by himself. I think he still is.

"And this has everything he needs, even a studio," she added.

"A studio?" Riley asked. "Why does Sam need a studio?"

"Because he paints," she said, turning to look at him. "He always has. But his work has changed. He used to paint landscapes in bright colors that made people smile and laugh. You've seen some of his work."

"I have?" Riley asked. "Where?"

"In the long hallway outside the gym in your school," she said, slowing down yet again as the already narrow road grew even tighter until branches brushed against the sides of the car, as if hands were reaching out to them in the darkness.

Riley thought of the mural, probably twenty-five feet long, painted on white cinderblock. He passed it several times every day and had admired it, even though the paint was chipped and missing in places. At one point someone must have scribbled something on it, because that spot was now covered with a stripe of white paint like a Band-Aid. The painting was a landscape full of rolling hills, brilliant green fields, woods, black-and-white cows, red barns, and low white houses. Although there wasn't anything in it specifically to tell anyone that it was Sharon, none of the landmarks like the library or the general store or even his own house on the green, Riley had known from the first time he saw it that it was this town, these hills.

"Sam did that?" Riley asked with surprise.

"When he was only sixteen," his mother said. "He was very talented. He wanted to go far."

They pulled into a clearing and stopped. The headlights illuminated a small log cabin, one story high with a porch on the front and a bent basketball hoop missing a net on a side that had no windows. Around the cabin, the yard was as tidy as an ironed handkerchief. Most of the front yard was a garden. Although nothing grew in it now, it had been carefully cleared for winter, and the soil rose in straight rows like buried logs. Against the windowless side of the cabin, below the basketball hoop, a long wall of wood was neatly chopped and stacked, weathered now to silver.

"Come on, let's unpack. It's cold out here," Riley's mother said as she pushed her door open and headed up the path of flat stones that was obviously the walk.

They carried in their few things and turned on lights to push away the dark woods. Inside, the cabin was spare but comfortable. A blue couch hugged an inside wall. Next to it was an end table piled with books and magazines. The book on top, Riley noticed, was titled *How to Master Chess*. Off to the side was an oak table varnished to a blinding shine. The only two chairs in the cabin faced each other across the table. The kitchen was barely big enough for one, but the cabinet doors were beautiful, made from some dark reddish wood and lighter, grooved panels. There were only three lamps and there was no television, but a portable radio was plugged in on the kitchen counter. Through one of the three doorways, Riley could see the foot of a bed draped in a patchwork quilt. None of the windows had curtains, but Riley guessed there wasn't much need for them out here.

"There's only the one bed," Riley's mother said, "but Sam said there's a couch in the studio, through that door." She pointed to a dark doorway.

Riley went in and groped for the light switch. When the lights came on, he jumped. Large canvases, four and five and six feet tall, were stacked against the walls. There must have been ten or twenty of them. Each one was smeared with dark paint, navies and black, grays and browns. Here and there was a spot of color, yellow perhaps, or white. All of the paint had been slathered on in gobs, disturbing puddles of color that ran and slithered in streaks toward the floor.

"Unsettling, isn't it?" said his mother behind him. He turned to see her leaning against the door frame, her face as sad as he had ever seen it.

"What are they?" Riley demanded. He wasn't sure he could sleep in here with all this violent energy pulsing in the room's small space.

"You must promise never to tell anyone," his mother said. "Sam trusts you, or he would never have let you come here."

"Tell what?" Riley insisted. "What is this?"

"Well, Sam never said as much, but I knew right away when I saw them what they were," his mother said. "They're tears."

❧ *Chapter* EIGHT

The next day, when Riley let himself in through the kitchen door after school, he was greeted by a rush of warm air. Everything seemed back to normal except for the basil over the sink, which was brown and withered. Riley carried the pot outside and put it beside the steps.

The day after that Sam came for Thanksgiving dinner. He brought red pepper relish and squash casserole.

"I made these both myself, with my own maple syrup," he told them, "so I couldn't be accused of coming empty-handed to the feast."

"Did you make the maple syrup this fall?" Riley asked. It sounded like something he might be interested in learning.

Sam laughed. "Nope. You make maple syrup at the end of the winter, when you can just about see spring coming but it's not there yet. If you want to help, I'll remember that."

Riley made a mental note to put aside all his questions about Sam for one day while he ate. He also pledged to himself to try some of Sam's cooking, just to see what it was like, but his mouth was watering for turkey, a genuine piece of white meat tender enough to melt in his mouth and slathered with gravy.

"I'm making turkey especially for you," his mother had said late that morning with a smile. For the next four hours she was diligent about basting the bird every fifteen minutes. Every time she opened the oven door, Riley was ready to eat right then. Finally, the three of them sat down to eat in the late afternoon. Riley's mother turned to him.

"Would you like to say grace, Riley?" she asked.

Riley looked across the table at Sam, the man who looked like Jesus. His hands, the ones that looked like Jesus' hands in prayer, were clasped together beneath his chin, waiting. Riley couldn't say right then how he felt about Sam. He was grateful that Sam had taken some of the burden off him for being the only one his mother had left. He didn't feel as if he had to be everything anymore. And it was clear that Sam's company made his mother happy. She laughed more and talked more, in ways that seemed familiar to him but distant, almost beyond memory.

But it wasn't that simple. Riley knew that Sam and he were alike in ways that sometimes made him uncomfortable. Neither one of them was very pushy, for example. They were both on the quiet side, and Sam was smart, too, although he didn't go out of his way to broadcast it. But Riley also looked at Sam as the one who was making it harder and harder for his mother to leave Sharon again. And he was ashamed of Sam for turning tail in Vietnam and leaving when other men were dying. Thousands of them weren't sitting down to Thanksgiving dinner with their families today. A few painted tears weren't going to change that.

"No," he said. He didn't offer any explanation.

His mother looked surprised, but she didn't push.

"I will," Sam volunteered. He bowed his head.

"Dear Lord, thank you for all that we have. Help us to share those things we have in abundance and to be better people than we really are. Help us to forgive others and to walk in the paths of righteousness without judging others. Amen."

When Riley looked up, Sam was smiling his shy smile at him. "Why don't you pass the turkey to your mother," he said. "If she starts with her own cooking, maybe she'll be too full to notice mine."

Later, when they were clearing the table, Sam asked Riley, "You know Mary St. Francis, don't you? Isn't she in your class at school?"

"I know her," Riley said, wondering why Sam asked.

"If you're not doing anything tomorrow, how about going down to her place and helping her stack wood? She's got three cords of wood to move."

"I don't know where she lives," Riley said. He wasn't eager to help anyone stack wood, especially a girl, even if he had decided that he liked her.

"I'll take you down in my truck. Be ready around nine—although Mary will already have been at it for a couple of hours before you get there."

And so it was all settled, even though Riley wanted no part of it, just like apprenticing.

Sam arrived closer to eight-thirty and stood in the kitchen drinking coffee with Riley's mother while Riley got ready.

"Wear warm clothes, but wear them in layers," he called out. "That way you can peel off clothes as you get hot. And you will get hot. Stacking wood is hard work."

It's freezing out there, Riley thought to himself as he put on a heavy wool sweater and his jacket. How stupid could Sam be to think he could possibly get hot enough to want to take anything off? Before he had time to answer that, Sam called up once more from the bottom of the stairs.

"And don't forget gloves."

When Riley finally came back into the kitchen, Sam looked at the thin knitted gloves that were hanging out of his pocket.

"Don't you have anything heavier?" Sam asked.

"No," Riley said petulantly. "We didn't stack much wood in Stony Point." The sarcasm appeared to be lost on Sam.

"Go get in the truck," Sam said. "I'll be right there."

Sam came out in less than a minute and climbed into

the driver's seat. The truck came to life with the sound of a chainsaw, and Sam drove the two hundred yards to the general store.

"Wait here," he ordered.

Who does he think he's bossing around? Riley complained to himself. Go there, stack wood, put your coat on, stay here. He was tempted to get out of the truck just to make the point, but that didn't make any sense. He would just have to get in again when Sam came back. So in spite of the cold, he rolled down the window and propped his elbow on the door just as he would have done if it had been ninety degrees in the shade.

When Sam returned, he climbed into the truck and tossed a pair of canvas gloves into Riley's lap.

"Wear those," he said. "They'll keep you from getting splinters."

As they drove off, west out of town, cold air flooded the truck cab from the open window.

"You sure you want that window open?" Sam asked.

"It was feeling stuffy in here. I wanted some fresh air," Riley lied. He had clearly miscalculated, and he badly wanted to close the window, but he thought he could tough it out until they arrived at Mary's house. He just hoped that her house was nearby.

"Oh, I imagine you'll get your fill of fresh air today," Sam said, and then he didn't say another word until they reached the edge of the village.

Sam turned off on a dirt road and went about fifty yards, down a lane of crowded fir trees and over a small bridge, up to a dilapidated blue-and-white trailer where Riley discovered that three cords of wood made a mountain that looked as if it belonged in the Himalayas. In spite of himself, he caught his breath. Broken bicycles, tires, a dented washing machine that wasn't connected to anything, and a rusted set of bedsprings littered the yard. A crooked chimney pipe poked through the flat roof, and near one corner of the trailer a large rust spot spread over the side as if it were lava flowing off the roof.

Mary was hard at work filling up a canvas sling with logs. When Sam stopped, she stood up and smiled.

"Hi, Mary," Sam called. "I brought you some help." He turned to Riley. "Go on, get out. She can use all the help you can give her."

Riley opened the door and jumped to the ground.

"Hello," he said awkwardly.

"Mary will show you what to do. She's a pro at this," Sam said. "I'll come by around four. Even if you're not done, you'll be ready to quit by then." He waved once more to Mary and leaned across the seat and rolled up the window. Then he turned around and drove his rattly truck back over the bridge toward town, leaving a cold blue cloud of exhaust behind.

They both stood there wordless for a minute.

Finally, Mary said, "Thanks for coming to help. I've

been doing this by myself for two years. Claire's too little to do more than get in the way. But it's an awful lot of work, and I hate it! I'm so tired by the end of the weekend that I can't go to school on Monday."

"I didn't volunteer," Riley said. "Sam made me come."

"Sam Mitchell's a good man," Mary said.

"That's the second time you've told me that," Riley said impatiently. "What does Sam have to do with this?"

"It's his wood," Mary said. She was surprised and clearly confused. "He brings all this wood each fall, even though nobody asks him to, and dumps it in the front yard."

"Why?" Riley asked.

"Because we'd probably freeze without it," Mary said. "Sometimes my father pays the oil bill and sometimes he doesn't. Sometimes we don't have enough money to pay for oil. Then we burn Sam's wood."

Riley looked over toward the listing trailer. It sat on cinderblocks that may once have been straight and level but weren't anymore. The front door didn't even look like it closed tightly. He found it hard to believe that a family could live there. He found it harder to believe that Mary, the Mary whom he sometimes thought was the only other kid in the whole town of Sharon who wanted to learn anything, could live in a place like this.

"Why does he do it?" Riley asked.

"I don't know. I never asked him. I just say thank you."

"Where's your father?" Riley asked.

"I don't know," Mary said. "He has problems. We don't always know where he is. He wouldn't be any help with this anyway."

"Why not?" Riley asked. It seemed to him as he looked at the pile of wood that a grown man would be a big help.

"He can't lift things. He has shrapnel in his back," Mary explained.

"Shrapnel?" Riley asked. "How'd he get that?"

"In Vietnam," Mary said. "He was in the hospital for two years. He and Sam came home about the same time. I was little. It seems like a long time ago, but not to him."

"Where's Claire?" Riley asked, looking around. He was confused by how different and strange everything seemed here, almost as if this dilapidated trailer and the dirt road that led to it weren't part of the same town he was living in.

"At a friend's. I knew I'd be busy all weekend with the wood," Mary said. She pointed to the pile, which was almost as tall as they were and at least fifteen feet long, as if the pile spoke for itself.

"Where's your mother?" Riley asked.

"In the trailer, watching TV. That's all she ever does," Mary said.

"Do you have other brothers or sisters?" Riley asked.

"No," Mary said. "Is that everything?"

"No," said Riley. "Why do you have to stack the wood?

Why can't you just leave it in a big pile in the front yard and take a log off every time you need one?"

"Because it would get buried under the snow and get wet and then smoke when we needed to burn it," Mary explained. She leaned over and grasped the handles of the canvas sling. "Come on, I'll show you where it goes."

"I'll take that," Riley said. He stepped forward and took the handles from Mary and almost fell over because he had been expecting something much lighter. Mary hadn't even stooped under the load, but Riley struggled to look nonchalant as he adjusted to the weight. She struck off for a shed at the corner of the trailer and Riley staggered behind. All at once the day stretching out before them took on a new aspect. He had figured it was going to be awkward, but it had never occurred to him to worry about his arms being pulled from their sockets.

Riley had shed his jacket by ten. When noon came, he had shed his sweater, too, and his arms were throbbing as if they were broken. Even worse, the pile of wood in the yard hardly looked any smaller than it had at nine o'clock. Somehow, though, the shed was filling up with neat rows of wood.

Mary threw her wood carrier down.

"Come on," Mary said. "I'll fix us something for lunch."

She headed for the trailer's front door.

Riley was too weary to do more than follow along behind. As he climbed the front steps, he noted that they were in worse shape than the ones Sam had fallen through at his house. He could not believe the inside of the trailer. Behind the drawn curtains, a sort of permanent twilight cast a pall over everything. The furniture comprised a torn brown couch the color of mud and an oversized orange recliner. A gaudy afghan in pink and green had been tossed haphazardly over the couch cushions, as had a big pillow, as if someone had recently been sleeping there.

Mary followed Riley's eyes. "That's my Dad's bed. Mom says he thrashes around so much at night she can't get any sleep at all."

But Mrs. St. Francis didn't look to Riley as if she did enough to need much rest. She was sitting dully in the recliner in front of the television, her faced bathed in blue light from the screen. A cigarette dangled from her mouth. The floor around her chair was littered with a cigarette box and candy wrappers. She looked up when Mary and Riley came in and nodded, but she didn't say anything. She didn't seem the least bit curious about who Riley was or why he was there.

"What are you watching, Mom?" Mary asked, making no effort to introduce Riley. She walked over and picked up the candy wrappers.

"*Green Acres,*" said Mrs. St. Francis. She removed her cigarette from her mouth and blew out a cloud of blue smoke. "Damn reruns."

"You've probably seen them all by now, Mom," Mary

said. "I'm going to fix us some lunch. Do you want anything?"

But Mrs. St. Francis had already returned her attention to the television. The chatter and music from it made talk unneccessary, and for that Riley was grateful.

Mary searched the cupboards and found a can of pea soup and some peanut butter. She took a pan off a shelf and washed it.

"Why are you washing it if it's already clean?" Riley asked.

"Mice," Mary said.

Riley nearly lost his appetite then and there, but he was starving. In addition, he wanted lunch to last as long as possible, maybe until next Tuesday or Wednesday, when he thought his arms might begin to feel normal again. Unfortunately, after they'd eaten the soup and a peanut butter sandwich without anything on it, there was nothing to do but go back to work.

Through much of the afternoon they carried their loads in silence. Riley hadn't worn his watch, but when the light finally started to fade, he was afraid Sam might have forgotten him. It *had* to be later than four. He had never been so tired in his life. The pile of wood, however, was almost gone. Riley wondered what trick of the mind had kept it from shrinking in the morning, despite all their energy and work, and let it melt away in the afternoon, when both of them were dead tired and slow.

When Sam finally pulled in, he rolled down his window.

"Looks great, Mary!" he called to her. "You two have earned a good night's sleep tonight. Climb in, Riley."

"I can't yet," he said. "We have two loads left and then it'll be done. I want to finish."

So Sam kept the truck idling in the driveway, coughing its blue exhaust, while Mary and Riley each made two more trips, their arms now as heavy as cinderblocks.

"Thanks," Mary said as she walked Riley back to the truck. "I never had any help before. I never got it done in one day. It'll be awfully nice not to have to carry more wood tomorrow."

"Sure," Riley said. He was feeling very uncomfortable. He found it hard to believe that Mary had carried all that wood by herself in years past, when she was younger and smaller. But he had barely kept up with her today, so maybe it was true.

"I'll see you in school on Monday," she said.

"Yeah, okay," Riley said, surprised that the prospect of seeing her there pleased him. "I guess that will be a first—I mean, you being in school on a Monday after stacking your wood pile."

Mary smiled.

Riley climbed into the truck beside Sam, who tooted the horn once and drove off, his truck rattling like a box of dropped tools.

"How did those gloves work out?" Sam asked when they reached the main road.

Riley looked at his hands and was surprised to see that he was wearing the gloves, probably had been all day, except when he took them off to eat lunch. Everything below his shoulders was numb with the strain of carrying a couple of tons of wood. He couldn't even feel his hands.

"Fine. Great. Thanks," Riley mumbled, too tired to make much effort to converse.

"That was a good thing you did today," Sam said. "Mary St. Francis is a brave and remarkable girl. You would be lucky to have her as a friend."

Riley slumped in his seat, exhausted and beyond responding. Sam Mitchell, what would you know about being brave and remarkable? he wondered.

When Riley got home, he staggered past his mother and went directly upstairs to bed. His mother came up a few minutes later.

"Are you okay?" she asked. "We're having pizza for dinner. Don't you want some?"

"Only if you'll feed me," Riley said, but the bed was so soft and the covers so warm that he decided not to bother staying awake until the pizza arrived.

✳ *Chapter* NINE

The next day, thank goodness, his mother left him alone. Riley hardly moved off the couch except to eat. His arms ached whenever he moved them, and he moved them as little as possible. He hoped Mary was feeling at least as bad so he could keep some of his self-respect. He believed it would not have been possible for him to carry wood today, even if someone had put a gun to his head.

In the afternoon, Sam took a break from sanding the old wood floor in Riley's mother's bedroom.

"Want to play chess?" Sam offered.

"No, thanks," Riley said. He was curious to know what Sam had picked up from his book, but the truth was he couldn't face the prospect of moving his arms.

By the next day, though, the sound of the sander whining incessantly upstairs drove him outside.

He took the binoculars from the top of his dresser, where he kept them standing on a towel so he could admire them every night for a couple of minutes before he turned off the light, and put on his brown jacket. From his house to the woods up the road was no more than a quarter of a mile. The woods looked stark and thick, not at all like the woods he'd known in Stony Point, which were really no more than a stand of trees and bramble in Bobby Opel's backyard. When the leaves were off the trees there, you could see right through them to the rail-road tracks, so while it had given them a place to play, he had never thought of it as wild. He followed the asphalt until he reached the line of trees, and then he turned off the road and plunged into the woods.

There weren't any railroad tracks here. There wasn't much of anything if you didn't count the trees and a lit-tle brush. And there was very little brush. It felt almost like a cathedral with a dense tangle of branches overhead and down below the trees growing thick and straight as columns. He had never been alone in real woods before, and his senses were on full alert. The air was still and al-most sweet, full of the fragrance of damp earth and rot. As he walked, his footsteps sounded like small explo-sions as each footfall crushed the brittle brown leaves that carpeted the ground. Nothing moved, except a few birds flitting about in the dim light. He was disappointed not to see more signs of wildlife. He was hoping for a glimpse of a moose, maybe a bear.

He walked for half an hour before he started to worry about finding his way back. Two or three times he stopped to look through his binoculars. Once he studied a huge hole high up in a tree, at the base of which was a pile of wood shavings. Thanks to the binoculars, he could study the way the hole had been chipped from the trunk of the tree, but he couldn't see anything in the hole, and he had no idea what would make such a hole.

It gave him a thrill to handle Silas Griffin's field glasses. He loved the feel of the cool metal in his hands, even though Sam had told him that the Battle of Gettysburg was fought on days that were hot and humid, when the binoculars would have been warm and sticky in his great-great-great-grandfather's hands as he scouted out the Confederates a mile or more away. Though the fighting had been over for 117 years, Vermont was still proud of its part, and Riley had a piece of that history hanging around his neck as he tramped through the dead leaves. Someone he knew, or almost knew, or practically knew, had used them to help save his country when it was in danger. Riley patted the binoculars from time to time just to reassure himself that they were real and they were his.

For a hundred yards he followed an old wall laid up with stones the size of a man's head. It was tumbled down and covered in places with lichen and moss, but it still cut a straight line over the earth's bumps and depressions. At the end of it, he discovered a stone foundation. Whatever had once stood above it had long since collapsed into the cellar hole and mostly rotted away. It spooked Riley to think that people had once been here, so deep in the woods, and after he had glanced around quickly, thinking how much its isolation reminded him of Sam's cabin, he started back, looking over his shoulder regularly until the foundation was lost in the trees.

He was making his way back along the course he thought he had taken and was coming upon a small clearing when he heard something. His head snapped up, his heart hammering like a drum. His eyes swept the woods—all around him a monotonous study of tree trunks and dead leaves—searching for the source of the sound. His ears led him to the noise finally: Three enormous birds, mottled brown and black and big as vultures. If not for their red wattles, he would have been afraid they really were vultures.

The wild turkeys were scrabbling in the leaves thirty yards away in a place where the trees thinned out. Every once in a while, one of them would lift its white head, its bright red wattle swinging under its chin, and swivel its neck as if it were sniffing the air. All the while, they kept up a regular conversation, murmuring gobbles like water running over stones in a brook.

Riley didn't try to get any closer. He quietly took up a position, bracing himself against a tree. Slowly, he reached up and took off his glasses and stuffed them in his pocket. Then just as slowly he raised his binoculars to his eyes.

The turkeys filled the circles of his lenses. Even from this distance, he could see individual dark brown feathers striped with white along their wings and the rough, bumpy texture of their wattles. Their beaks pushed the leaves aside like ice cutters as they pushed their way through the dry underbrush.

When Riley's arms finally tired, he had to lower them. As he did so, he knocked his glasses out of his pocket. It was when he leaned over to pick them up that he heard the shot and almost instantaneously the thwack of a bullet slamming into the tree beside his head.

He screamed and fell to the ground as if he had been hit. In fact, he could not tell whether he had been hit. The turkeys lifted off in a wild scramble, their hysterical gobbles drowning out all other sound.

Riley was crying, cowering in a ball, when he heard, "Judas Priest! Kid, are you hit?" He felt a hand on his back trying to roll him over.

Riley raised his head, although it felt disconnected, as if it might float away by itself. He was sobbing and panting and gulping air as if he could never get enough of it.

Tim Ferris, his face white as a sheet, hovered over him, gripping a rifle.

A man knelt by Riley's side. His eyes were frantic with concern.

"Kid, are you hurt? Are you okay?" the man pleaded.

"I think so," Riley whimpered, trying to stop crying. He didn't want Tim to see him like this, although Tim hardly looked better himself.

The man put his hand under Riley's elbow and gently helped him to his feet. Riley was terrified. His thigh felt cold and wet, and when he looked down he was ashamed to discover that his crotch was dark with a wet stain. He didn't remember peeing, but it was obvious he had.

"Judas H. Priest, Tim! What the hell did you think you were shooting at?" the man demanded. The relief in his face flooded out like anger.

Tim's face was still as white as Riley imagined his was.

"I saw something move. It was big. I-I-I thought it was a deer," Tim stammered. His hands seemed frozen on the barrel of his gun.

"Did you see antlers?" The man was relentless. He took a step toward Tim. "Did you see a white tail?"

"All I saw was something brown moving, Dad. I figured what else would be out in the woods that was big and brown," Tim whined, almost in tears himself.

For the first time, Riley noticed that Tim and his father both wore bright orange vests like the ones that hung on racks down at the Sharon General Store.

"Well, look at him, Dad," Tim pleaded. "Look how he's dressed. How am I supposed to tell him apart from a deer?"

"That's his foolishness," Mr. Ferris said, "but if you had killed him, it would have been your fault."

Mr. Ferris had been studying the ground, and now he raised his eyes and found the bullet lodged in the tree trunk. He took a knife from a sheath on his belt and pried it out. He handed the flattened slug to Tim.

"You hold on to that," he ordered his son. "I want it to be a constant reminder to you that you damn near killed someone because you were careless."

"But Dad," Tim insisted, his voice stronger than before and growing stronger with every protest, "he's an idiot. Look at him! It's deer season—as if everyone doesn't know—and he's out in the woods in a brown coat. No red, no orange, nothing to protect him."

"Be that as it may," Mr. Ferris said, "you just can't shoot without knowing what you're shooting at."

Mr. Ferris turned to Riley. "Can you walk?" His glance covered Riley head to foot, and Riley could tell he was noticing for the first time Riley's wet pants.

"Good," he said with relief. "Let's go. We'll walk you out. You shouldn't be in the woods this time of year without wearing something bright. You were damn lucky."

"But Dad," Tim protested. "Are we stopping? It's the last day of deer season. You said we'd stay out until it turned dark or we got something. You promised."

"You thank your lucky stars you didn't get anything today, son," Mr. Ferris said.

"I need my glasses," Riley stammered. "I was trying to pick them up."

Tim didn't move, but Mr. Ferris helped Riley push around the leaves until they found them. To Riley's amazement and relief, the glasses were fine, not even bent.

"Come on," Mr. Ferris said to both boys. "I've had enough for today."

After they'd taken the first few steps, Riley wished he had asked to sit down for a few minutes. His breathing was still fast and shallow, and even small steps seemed to take away what little breath he had. His damp legs were cold, and he wished the earth would open up and swallow him.

They had walked for ten minutes, silently except for the rustle of leaves under their feet, when Mr. Ferris asked, "What were you doing out there, kid?"

"Just looking at things," Riley said sheepishly.

"Through those?" Mr. Ferris, asked, pointing at Riley's binoculars. "What are they anyway?"

"They belonged to my great-great-great-grandfather," Riley explained, glad to have a conversation topic other than being shot at and peeing in his pants.

"They must be pretty old," Mr. Ferris remarked. "Are they any good?"

"They're okay. I was looking at some wild turkeys," Riley said, regretting his words almost at once because they sounded so silly.

"You're out in the woods, in a brown jacket, during deer hunting season, looking at turkeys with a stupid pair of old binoculars," Tim sneered. "That's real smart."

"You watch yourself," Mr. Ferris said to his son. "What you did today was plenty dumb, too. I'd say you're about tied for idiocy this afternoon. You're lucky to be alive," he said, nodding toward Riley, "and Timothy, you'll be lucky if I ever take you deer hunting again. You probably both want to consider never mentioning this episode to anyone. You'd both look like fools."

"Aw, Dad," Tim wheedled, but his father silenced him with a look.

Riley kept his head down and put one foot in front of the other until they reached the edge of the trees.

"What's your name, kid?" Mr. Ferris asked.

"Riley Griffin, sir."

"You Kate's boy?" Mr. Ferris asked.

"Yes, sir."

"I went to school with your mother. I heard she had moved back. And that Sam Mitchell had come out of the woods to pick up where he left off," Mr. Riley said.

"I don't know much about that," Riley said. "He's helping us fix up the house."

Mr. Ferris chuckled.

"Well, I know you're just down the road there, and we're up here over the hill. Can you make it by yourself?"

Riley would have crawled before he let Tim Ferris escort him home.

"Yes, sir, I can."

"Tell Riley you're sorry, Tim," his father ordered.

"Dad, please," Tim begged.

"Just do it," Mr. Ferris said.

Tim lowered his head. "I'm sorry," he mumbled so low that Riley could barely hear it, but he didn't care. He had turned himself sidewise to Tim so he wouldn't have to face him with his pants still damp and stained with urine. As soon as Tim had finished speaking, Riley started for home.

"Stay out of the woods during deer hunting season, kid," Mr. Ferris called after him.

When he reached home, he was relieved to find a note from his mother on the counter.

"Sam and I have gone for a walk. Be back in a while."

Riley ran upstairs and stripped off his pants. Wadding them into a ball, he stuffed them into a plastic bag and buried them in the garbage can in the garage. Then he went back upstairs and shoved the binoculars deep into a drawer full of sweaters. After that, he climbed into bed. He sobbed for half an hour with his quilt pulled up over his head trying to get warm, but he couldn't stop shivering.

Chapter TEN

Snow was falling in big, wet flakes when Riley came down to breakfast before school on the Monday after Thanksgiving. The ground was already white, and the sky looked as if it had plenty more where that came from.

"If this snow stays," his mother said as she put a bowl of oatmeal and a glass of orange juice in front of Riley, "this will be the first day of winter."

"That's not until December twenty-first," Riley corrected her. He poured maple syrup over the oatmeal.

"In Vermont, winter starts when the snow falls for good," his mother said. "By the time December twenty-first arrives, you'll feel like it's been winter forever."

At school Riley avoided Tim Ferris, and Tim avoided him. Riley took that as a sign that Tim would keep his mouth shut. He sure would do the same.

On Tuesday Riley went to Mr. Aja's classroom after school. Mary and Mr. Aja were standing by the window, talking quietly.

"Mr. Griffin! This is perfect!" Mr. Aja said when he saw Riley in the doorway. "I have some reports to fill out. You can challenge the chess queen here."

Together, they played four games in two hours while darkness as black as ink descended outside. Several times Riley glanced up at the big blank windows and concluded that for some reason darkness was blacker here in Sharon, more absolute, than it had been back in Stony Point. It felt to him as if the world beyond the rim of hills had simply disappeared.

Mary won the first game, but he bested her in the next. Then Riley played against Mr. Aja and won. Finally, Mary played Mr. Aja and lost. No one talked much, but the mood was lighthearted and comfortable, and Riley found himself enjoying the company as much as the game itself. As Riley watched the last game unfold, he thought to himself, this is as happy as I have been in Sharon since the day Mom and I arrived.

"It was a good afternoon of play," Mr. Aja remarked as they put the chess set away. "Everyone was triumphant, and everyone had to eat some dirt. A little humility is good for the soul."

They walked outside, shutting off lights behind them, into the orange neon glow of the schoolyard spotlight, the one that shone into Riley's room every night.

"Good night, Riley. It was good to have you come today," Mr. Aja said. "I hope you'll become a regular. The chess club could use another member."

"Do you ever play in competition?" Riley asked.

"Once, in the spring, at the statewide match," Mr. Aja

said. "That's why we go through this rigorous work every week." He laughed at his own joke. "But seriously, Mary did very well last year, considering that her only practice was against me."

Riley looked to Mary to hear how she had placed, but she only lowered her head and stared at her shoes.

"Don't hide your light under a bushel, Mary," Mr. Aja said. "She came in third in the state in her age group. But Mary and I started playing two years ago for fun, and that's mostly why we continue. Come on, Mary, I'll give you a ride home."

✂   ✂   ✂

The next weekend Riley went with his mother to Montpelier, the state capital, forty minutes north of Sharon, to buy winter boots, warm gloves, and a parka. Nobody called them jackets here. Everyone had parkas, big bulky nylon coats stuffed with down that made the people who wore them look like astronauts ready to walk on the moon. Riley picked a bright blue one, one that could never, ever, be confused with a deer. It made him feel like a neon raspberry Popsicle, but it was warm and bright, and that was all he was beginning to care about as winter closed in around them. While they were in the tiny city, they went out to dinner and to the movies. It was the first time they'd shared such an outing since they arrived in Sharon in mid-August.

Two weeks before Christmas, the Sharon Garden

Club put up a fifteen-foot-tall fir tree on the green and strung it with colored lights. Every evening at four o'clock, as the heavy hand of night slapped down on them, someone plugged in the lights and helped chase away the winter gloom with a riot of twinkling color.

Riley's mother had been right. Christmas in Sharon was beautiful. A little snow fell almost every day, and while none of the snowfalls amounted to very much, the snow began to pile up. Along the walkway between the Griffins' porch steps and the garage, the drifts Riley shoveled came up almost to his waist. The houses all looked as if they were wearing white hats. Every door was decorated with a real wreath and different arrangements of plaid and red ribbons and pine cones. There weren't any fake wreaths, like the ones the Griffins had put on their door in Stony Point, the ones that came from the shopping mall already dripping with red plastic bows, gaudy gold balls, and fake snow and that spent every summer in the attic.

At night, looking down across the almost silent green lined with old houses, their windows twinkling warmly with light, and the town Christmas tree ablaze with color, Riley confessed to himself that he had never seen anything as pretty. One evening, after several inches of new snow had fallen, just at twilight, he heard bells and went to the window. As hard as it was to believe, someone was actually riding by in a sleigh. The horse was no more than a silhouette in the darkness, but he heard a woman's laugh as the sleigh came down the hill past their house and down along the green.

Shopping for his mother for Christmas was hard. The hunting jackets, fishing lures, children's toys—even the needles and thread—carried at the Sharon General Store didn't seem to fit his mother's tastes. Finally, he came up with the idea of giving her coupons. It wasn't original, but he told himself it was something he could do in a place where his shopping options ranged from mops to cans of baked beans and the house still needed lots of work. He had actually acquired a few skills apprenticing. He began working at night to put together a booklet with coupons good for work around the house: doing the dishes all by himself, scrubbing the bathroom, fixing a dinner, painting the pantry. By thinking hard, he managed to come up with ten chores he thought he could handle, as long as his mother didn't expect too much.

The Sunday afternoon before Christmas, he and his mother drove out to Sam's. It was Riley's first time back since they had spent the night there. Sam's road looked very different by daylight. The trees were still as erect as sentinels, but their branches looked like arms covered in thick white sleeves. When Riley entered the cabin, he was relieved to find the door to the studio closed, although the smell of paint and turpentine hung heavily in the air. Riley could imagine that behind the door there was a canvas, still wet and smeared with fresh browns and blacks, dripping rivulets of paint even as he and his mother and Sam sipped hot spiced cider and put on their hats and gloves to go out in the woods to cut down a tree.

Walking in the snow was hard work. The crust of the snow held Riley for a fraction of a second at every step, and then he broke through, crashing to the forest floor more than a foot below.

Fifteen minutes after they started tramping around studying the possibilities, Riley's mother said, "I have picked out the perfect tree."

Sam and Riley looked around. Her choice was not immediately apparent to Riley.

"Which one is it?" Sam asked. He sounded as confused as Riley felt.

"It's the best one near the house," she laughed. The color in her cheeks was high and her eyes sparkled with mischief.

This turned out not to be the biggest or the fullest tree Riley had seen, but he agreed that it was a practical choice. He and Sam sprawled in the snow at its base and pushed a crosscut saw back and forth, while the sharp smell of cut fir filled their nostrils and pine needles caught in their hair. Finally, the tree broke free from its stump.

Before they started dragging it back to the truck by

its trunk, Riley asked, "Shouldn't we cut one for you, Sam? Don't you want one for the cabin?"

"I haven't had a Christmas tree in nine years," Sam said quietly. "I'll just enjoy yours. But I have an idea— let's cut one for Mary and her family."

The one they picked was smaller and sure to fit in the trailer, but it had a perfect shape. Riley thought it looked like a Christmas tree out of a magazine.

Riley rode back into town in Sam's truck, keeping an eye on the trees out the back window to make sure they didn't bounce out of the truck bed. They made a brief detour down the snow-packed dirt road where the St. Francises lived, and when no one answered the door, they left the tree leaning against the front of the trailer.

"Shouldn't we leave a note or something?" Riley asked as Sam turned to walk back to the truck.

"It's Christmas," Sam said and smiled. "Let them think it's a miracle."

Back at the Griffins' house, Riley discovered what Sam called the First Law of Christmas Trees You Cut Yourself: they always look tiny in the woods and they always turn out to be enormous in the house. Before they managed to get the tree up and in its stand, they had to cut six inches off the top and a foot off the bottom so they could squeeze the angel in under the ceiling. While Sam and Riley worked on the tree, Riley's mother rummaged through the still unpacked boxes in one of the unheated upstairs bedrooms until she found the box containing their Christmas decorations.

It was getting late and darkness had fallen when Sam said, "You'll want to finish up here soon."

"Why?" Riley's mother asked.

"They have Christmas carols on the green at six on the Sunday evening before Christmas," Sam explained.

"They didn't do that when we were growing up here," his mother said. "When did that start?"

"Six, seven years ago," Sam said as he hung a few more ornaments on the upper branches of the tree.

"Well, I want to do one more thing before we go," Riley's mother said. "Riley, why don't you go upstairs and bring down that pretty colored paper chain you've been working on? I don't know why you've been working on it, but this seems like a perfect time to string it over the doorway. It's really gotten quite long."

"I can't," Riley protested. "That's not what it's for at all!"

"What's it for, then?" his mother asked.

Now he was trapped. He could not answer that question without hurting her badly. She would be stung if she knew how faithfully he had been adding links to that chain every night.

"All right," he finally said, and slowly went upstairs to unpin his chain from the walls.

"I've changed my mind," his mother said when he

came back downstairs. Riley was dragging the chain behind him in long colorful loops that whispered down the
steps like water falling over waterfalls. "I think we should
drape it along the stair railing. It's a dramatic railing, and
we don't have anything festive to put on it. I probably
should have tried to make a swag from pine boughs, but
I never thought of it until now, and now it's too late for
this year. I'd never get it done. I'll get some string."

The three of them strung Riley's paper chain up the
railing of the long staircase, tying it at intervals between
the balusters and letting it drape gracefully in between
the ties. Riley was the only one who didn't stop to admire
it. How am I going to continue to add links to it every
day? he wondered as he ran string through the loops and
tied them to the railing. Mom'll notice if it starts getting
longer. It annoyed him that his mother had confiscated
one of the most personal things he owned and had put
it to her own purpose, a purpose that had nothing what-
soever to do with *his* purpose for it.

Sam called from the living room.

"They're gathering," he said, nodding toward the
green. He held Kate's coat for her and handed her her
gloves and scarf. Riley pulled on his parka and boots.

"Aren't you coming?" he asked Sam when he didn't
see him making any motions toward getting ready.

"No," said Sam. "I'll wait here."

"But—" protested Riley.

"Riley, come along. They'll start without us," his mother said, giving him a gentle push toward the door.

On the green, perhaps fifty people had gathered for caroling. Riley was surprised to see Mary and Claire. They were standing off to the side. Riley worked his way around the other carolers to join them. Both sisters were shivering in their thin coats.

"How did you get here?" Riley asked, looking around for either Mary's mother or father and knowing by now that he would see neither.

"We walked," Mary said matter-of-factly.

"Someone gave us a twee today," Claire said, her eyes bright with excitement and delight.

"They just left it by the front door," Mary explained. "We don't have a real stand, but I'm going to saw off the lowest limbs and stick it in a bucket of wet sand."

"I'm going to make a papew chain," Claire said happily. "A big one, with lots of colows in it. Mawy said she would get me some papew at the stowe."

Riley forced himself to smile at Claire and rub the top of her head, and then he turned around to the carolers. He didn't want Mary to see the fire rising in his cheeks or the shame burning in his eyes.

✄   ✄   ✄

Christmas morning, Sam arrived in time for breakfast even before Riley had opened the presents in his stocking.

"Merry Christmas, Riley, Kate," he said as he came through the door. His right hand was weighed down by a large shopping bag.

"Merry Christmas, Sam," Riley's mother said, and then, to Riley's surprise, she stepped close to him and kissed him. There wasn't anything halfhearted about it, Riley noticed. It was a full kiss right on the lips. Sam put his arm around her for just a fraction of a second and then let go.

"Before we eat," he said, "let me get something else from the truck." And he went back out into the crisp, clear morning.

When he came in again, he was carrying an armful of split logs, the kind you burn in woodstoves and fireplaces. I've carried enough of that to know what it is, Riley thought. But where is he going to build a fire? The fireplace in the living room had been closed up for years, and no one had gotten around to changing that.

Sam walked through the kitchen and down the hallway into the living room.

"What are you doing?" Riley's mother asked, following close behind him.

"This is your Christmas present," Sam told her. "I'm going to build you a fire in the fireplace today."

"But it's closed up," she protested.

"Not anymore." He smiled at her. "I was up here every day for two weeks before Riley got out of school, checking it over, repointing some of the mortar where it needed it, and putting in a new damper so you can close it up when you're not using it. Ta-dah!" He reached up inside the old brick fireplace and pulled on a chain that Riley noticed for the first time was dangling down from heaven knows where. They felt cold air rush in at their feet.

"See if you can find some newspaper, Riley," Sam ordered as he knelt and started breaking small branches into still smaller twigs.

Within fifteen minutes, Sam had a fire blazing in the fireplace. He returned to his truck and came back in with a screen that he carefully placed in front of it.

"Let's eat," he said, rubbing his hands together with satisfaction.

When they returned to the living room after breakfast, the fire was as warm as a blanket, and the tower of logs that Sam had erected had settled in upon itself. Riley handed his mother his present. She opened it, and flipped through the coupons that Riley had stapled together, and clapped her hands.

"Both these presents—the fire and all these coupons," she said with a broad smile. "They're wonderful gifts. They are just what I need."

Then Riley's mother gave him her gift. She lifted it from under the massive tree, and Riley could tell from the way she picked it up with both hands that it was heavy. When she laid it in his lap, it had the solidity of stone.

"What is it?" Riley asked, unable even to guess what might take such a flat, square shape and weigh so much.

Riley's mother and Sam laughed.

"You'll have to open it, kiddo," his mother said.

It was a chessboard, a magnificent wooden chessboard. The light and dark squares were made of different woods, not painted, just stained to bring out the grain. The edges were rounded and sanded smooth as baby skin.

"I asked Sam to make it for you," she explained.

"It's beautiful," Riley said, at a loss for other words, and looking from one to the other.

"Glad you think so," Sam said. "Maybe we can play some more this winter. The winter gets pretty long and dark, in case you haven't noticed."

Riley's mother gave Sam the wood that her father had kept out in the garage for his own woodworking projects. He hadn't done anything with that wood for years, and in the loft of the garage there was a supply of cherry, oak, and walnut that had only aged and grown more beautiful with time.

Finally, Sam brought out his gift for Riley. As his other big gift had been flat and square, this one was tall and square. It was wrapped in bright paper the way a child might wrap a gift, wrinkled and held together with yards of tape.

"Careful with it," Sam warned as he handed it to Riley.

Riley unwrapped an empty wooden case with glass panels on all four sides and on the top.

"What is it?" Riley asked awkwardly.

"It's a display case for your binoculars," Sam explained. "This way you can look at them, but they won't get dusty."

Riley had no choice. He went upstairs and dug the binoculars out of his sweater drawer, where he had buried them after that awful encounter with Tim Ferris. They felt good in his hands again.

Sam showed Riley how to take the lid off and lower the binoculars inside. When Riley put the lid back on, he stepped back to admire the effect.

"They look like they should be in a museum," Riley said.

Sam grinned. "I wanted to help you protect them as if they were," he said. "Sometimes it's a gift to be able to let go of your history, but sometimes it's a gift to hold on to it."

❧ *Chapter* ELEVEN

After Christmas, Riley felt as if a door had closed. The temperature fell to twenty and thirty degrees below zero. Even for the short walk from his house to the school, he bundled up, zipping his parka to his chin, pulling a hat so far down over his ears that his forehead disappeared, and wrapping a scarf across his mouth. Nothing helped. The moisture from his breath froze on the scarf a minute after he closed the kitchen door behind him, and by the time he reached the school door the scarf was as stiff as plaster of Paris. Wherever he walked, he was conscious of the snow squeaking underfoot. Wet snow made the kind of sloppy noises Riley expected, but the dry squeak of bitterly cold snow surprised him. Sam had told him the sound came from snow crystals breaking underfoot, but Riley had a hard time believing that anything as beautiful, small, and delicate as a snowflake could possibly complain this loudly.

For the most part, however, it didn't snow. Too cold to snow, Riley heard the people at the store saying, and that seemed as absurd as anything Sam had said. How could it be too cold to snow? All he could do was shake his head at nonsense like that. But even if he couldn't believe what they said, he noticed how they said it. They seemed to be proud of their circumstances, as if they had some special purchase on grit that made them better than other people. He had to admit they were certainly tougher than most of the people he had known back in Stony Point. You only had to look at their rough hands to realize that. But he hadn't decided yet whether they were better.

When the Christmas decorations came down in the middle of January, Riley's mother handed him his paper chain and thanked him for lending it to them for the holidays. Riley carried it back to his bedroom and laid it in giant coils on his bed. What should he do with it? he wondered. He had not added a single link to it since it had been confiscated to decorate the stairwell, although he had faithfully put aside strips of paper every day to add to it later, until one day he forgot. Then he forgot a couple of days. Soon the chain stopped representing the history it had been invented to record. One day Riley realized he didn't really know how many days he was behind. He could figure it out. He could look at the calendar and count backward to the Sunday before Christmas, but he didn't bother.

Now he looked at the chain lying on his bed and wondered what to do with it. He would put it back up, he finally decided, and he would add ten links to it just as a record of his continuing unhappiness in Sharon, but just to be fair, he wouldn't add links for the days when he had enjoyed himself. He was thinking particularly of Christmas and of the day he had gone into the woods with his mother and Sam to cut their tree, and of another day after New Year's when Sam had taken the two of them ice skating on a pond north of town. Then he remembered the afternoon of playing chess in Mr. Aja's room and how happy he had been then. When Riley pinned the chain back up in the corners of his room, he tore the last link off. He just remembered the good time he had had New Year's Day, when Sam took him snowshoeing in the woods behind his cabin and pointed out dozens of deer tracks in the snow under a gnarled apple tree.

"Why are they all here?" Riley had asked, looking around, secretly hoping to catch sight of a deer.

"It's a deer yard," Sam explained, "a place where deer can find something to forage on at this time of year."

"What's here besides the old apples?" Riley had asked. He looked closely at the shriveled, frozen apples and couldn't say that any of them looked very appetizing.

"Salt," Sam said, reaching into the trampled snow and uncovering a large block of white salt. "I put it here for them. They need it in the winter. Plus the deer feel safe here." He gestured with his mittened hand at the thick woods garlanded in white.

"Is that why you live out here?" Riley asked the question before he had even thought about it.

"In part, I guess," Sam admitted. "When I came home from Vietnam, I needed a long time by myself to begin to come to terms with what I had done. And I've stayed out here partly because I've grown accustomed to it and like being self-sufficient, and partly because some of the people in Sharon still haven't come to terms with what I did."

"Do you ever hunt?" Riley had asked then, shuddering as he recalled his near-miss in the woods and thinking of the gutted deer sprawled in the truck at the general store.

"Never," Sam had said. "I couldn't. I couldn't kill then, and I can't kill now."

⚔ ⚔ ⚔

The first Tuesday after school started, Riley went home promptly afterward and came back to Mr. Aja's class with his new chessboard.

"That's a beauty!" Mr. Aja said. He held it up to admire it better and whistled. "That is simply gorgeous. Almost too nice to play on, wouldn't you say, Miss St. Francis?"

"Did Sam make that?" Mary asked.

Riley nodded.

"My father says that if Sam Mitchell isn't good for anything else, he's a hell of a fine carpenter," Mary said suddenly.

Both Mr. Aja and Riley turned to stare at her. Neither one of them could say anything.

"Well, it's true," Mary stammered. "I mean, about the carpentry."

"Yes, I'd say that part is true." Mr. Aja laughed. "Sam Mitchell is one hell of a carpenter. Now, let's see what kind of chess player you are when you're forced to play on some of Mr. Mitchell's handiwork. You two play first. I'll watch."

Riley won every game that afternoon. He felt as if the board were blessed with magic powers.

✗   ✗   ✗

By late January the school was gearing up for the Groundhog Day Talent Show.

"What is it?" Riley asked Mary during lunch one day.

"It's sort of an annual ritual," she said. She finished the last bite of her peanut butter sandwich and drank the last of her carton of milk. That was all the lunch she ever had, Riley had noticed. Occasionally, he told her he wasn't interested in his apple or orange, and she always accepted it and ate it eagerly. "I think people just get bored with being indoors," she went on. "The school puts on a big talent show. Anyone who wants to perform can, and everybody in town comes."

"Do you perform?" Riley asked. He couldn't picture Mary on the stage being lighthearted.

Mary laughed. "No, I don't have any talents. Claire wants to, though. She says she wants me to make her a costume and she wants to sing 'I'm a Little Teapot.'"

Riley laughed too. "Are you going to?"

"Going to what?" Mary asked.

"Make her a costume? Let her perform?" Riley said.

"Of course," Mary said with surprise. "I don't know what I'll make a costume out of, but I'll come up with something."

Riley felt, like Mary, that he had no particular talent to share, but everyone else seemed gifted or at least bold enough to appear onstage in front of the whole town. Riley had never seen spirits at the school so high. Almost every afternoon he could hear the band practicing. Members of the chorus came in early to rehearse before school started in the morning. He even heard that Tim and his bunch of goons were going to perform some wrestling—as if that takes any special skill on their part, Riley thought.

Two days before the show, Mr. Aja asked if Mary and Riley would be willing to be the color guard, bearing the American and Vermont flags into the gymnasium at the start of the evening for the Pledge of Allegiance. Sure, they said, why not.

The night of the talent show, Riley came down for dinner dressed in jeans and a sweater.

"You can't wear that," his mother said as she stirred a big pot of chili.

"What's wrong with it?" Riley asked, looking down to

see if he had holes in the knees of his pants or a big stain on the front of his sweater.

"No jeans for the color guard," his mother said firmly.

He ended up wearing navy blue pants and a light blue shirt, and he was glad of it when he arrived at the school and found Mary wearing a faded cotton dress. She was shivering in her short sleeves, but Riley could tell that she had taken pains to dress up. Her hair, hanging down her back, shone like coal.

"Daddy is going to lead the Pledge of Allegiance," she said proudly.

"Why?" Riley asked, curious about why he would be assigned that honor. He adjusted the American flag he was holding in the harness that was draped around his neck.

"Because he's a war hero," she said. "Didn't you know?"

"No," said Riley. "What did he do?"

"He has a Purple Heart," she said, obviously surprised that Riley had not heard this story. "He saved his platoon from getting blown to bits by the Vietcong. He covered them while they escaped an ambush. That's how he got hurt. That's why he has shrapnel in his back."

Just then Mr. Stewart, the principal, started tapping on the microphone. Explosions of sound drifted over the crowd in the gymnasium that doubled as the auditorium. Everyone in town seemed to be there, Riley noted.

Everyone but Sam. Metal chairs clanged restlessly on the floor until people had made themselves comfortable. Gradually, silence descended except for the occasional cough.

"Thank you, thank you," Mr. Stewart said, his voice booming. "It's good to see everyone out on this cold night. We have a great program lined up for you. But first, the color guard will bring in the flags and we will say the Pledge of Allegiance."

Riley and Mary looked at each other and stepped out, and as they did so, the entire audience rose to its feet. When they reached the stage, they split, each one taking stairs at opposite sides of the stage. They rejoined and turned to face the audience.

"Stanley St. Francis is going to lead us in the Pledge of Allegiance," Mr. Stewart said, and nodded to someone offstage.

In a moment, Mr. St. Francis limped in from the wings. He was dressed in a wrinkled brown suit and his shirt collar was frayed, but it was clear to Riley that he, too, had taken pains to dress for the occasion. As soon as he saw Riley, he stopped.

"What the hell is he doing here?" he demanded in a voice loud enough to be heard in the back row. He pointed an unsteady finger at Riley.

There was a gasp in the audience.

"If you will just lead us in the pledge, Stan, we'll get

on with the show," Mr. Stewart said nervously. "I know everyone is looking forward to it."

A moment passed before Riley figured out that Mr. St. Francis was talking about him. What had he done?

"I won't say anything as long as that boy who's friends with that son-of-a-bitch Mitchell is holding the flag!" Mr. St. Francis shouted.

The audience was as silent as death.

"Come on, Stan, the boy has nothing to do with it," Mr. Stewart entreated.

Riley wanted to die. His knew his face was white and his hands on the flagpole were so wet he thought he might drop the flag.

"Daddy," Mary spoke up. "Please. Say the pledge. It's just Riley. He's my friend. It's not Sam."

Mr. St. Francis fixed his watery eyes on his daughter.

"It's the principle, damn it," he said. "The man's a coward and no patriot, and everybody knows it."

"Here, take it," Riley said, afraid that he was going to cry in front of all these people. "Just take it." He pulled the flag out of its holster and handed it to Mr. Stewart, who, surprised, fumbled it and nearly dropped it.

Mary's eyes were swimming with tears, too.

In an instant, Riley heard Mr. Aja start the pledge. *"I pledge allegiance to the flag . . ."*

There was nothing for Mr. St. Francis to do but slap his right hand over his chest and join in, as if it had been his idea all along to get started. In two seconds, the whole audience was reciting the pledge in a ragged unison.

When the pledge ended, Mr. Stewart handed the flag back to Riley and ushered the two flagbearers off the rear of the stage even though they were supposed to put the flags in their stands and march back out. The kindergarten teacher took the microphone and began announcing the first performances.

Riley was stunned.

"I'm so sorry," Mary pleaded. "I didn't know he would do anything like that."

He looked at her. "What did I do?" he asked.

"Nothing, nothing." She was trying valiantly not to cry. "It's just that my daddy can't forget. My mother says that other men came home from Vietnam, but my daddy brought Vietnam home with him. He says he's paid his dues, but I'd sure like to know when Mommy and Claire and I have paid enough, too."

Mr. Aja appeared. "You handled that very, very well," he said. "You should be very proud of yourselves."

"What did I do?" Riley demanded to know. Now that he had had a minute to think about it, he regretted giving up the flag so easily, especially in front of all those people. His face turned red with anger and humiliation, and he found his fists clenched as tightly as knots.

"Nothing," Mr. Aja assured him. "You are friends with someone who desperately needs a friend. That is nothing to be ashamed of. Now go out and enjoy yourselves. It's almost time for Claire's song."

They took the two seats that had been reserved for them in the first row, and Riley spent the evening feeling as if every eye in the gymnasium were boring a hole in his back.

Claire nearly brought the house down. She was dressed in a worn sheet that was gathered at her neck. One arm, the handle, poked out through a hole. The other arm was gracefully curved for the spout. She wore a big pot lid on her head. She sang in a sweet clear voice that echoed through the gym, and she never smiled, not once. She was the most serious teapot Riley had ever seen, but the audience loved her. Her teacher had to lead her back onto the stage for a second round of applause, which she received as stiffly as the first, because if she had bowed, her lid would have come crashing down.

Riley bolted for home as soon as the talent show ended.

"Riley, I am so sorry," his mother said as she swept into the kitchen close behind him. She took him in her arms and he did not protest.

"Sam would feel so bad if he knew what happened," she said. "But please don't tell him. He'll probably hear about it anyway, but please don't mention it."

"What was that all about?" Inside his shirt collar, Riley could feel his neck burning, still red with shame.

"It's a small town, a very small town," his mother said. "Feelings can run very deep, and even though these events are almost ten years old, you can see that some people have not forgotten them. They probably never will."

"But how could Mr. St. Francis still be so upset after all these years?" Riley asked. Ten years, after all, was almost his entire life.

"Mr. St. Francis will never understand what Sam did. We just have to accept that," his mother replied.

"I don't think that *I* can accept what Sam did," Riley retorted as he stomped upstairs to his room.

ϡ *Chapter* TWELVE

By mid-February it was clear that spring would eventually return. The light grew blue in the afternoon and stayed later every day. The sun shone more, and though the snow continued to fall, sometimes a foot at a time, the drifts on the south sides of houses and barns began to shrink from the newfound heat of the trapped light. Just a couple of days before everyone was to be released for February vacation, Mr. Aja made an announcement.

"Believe it or not," he said, "the end of the school year is coming fast upon us. Everyone must pick a topic in American history to research and write a short paper about. It will be due before April break. I want to know your topics by week's end so that the ambitious among you can get some work done over the vacation."

When class ended, Riley made his way to the front of the room to Mr. Aja's desk.

"What is it, Mr. Griffin?" Mr. Aja asked genially as he erased the blackboard.

"I have an idea for my research topic," Riley said.

"I thought you and possibly one other among the

general rabble of the class might enjoy this assignment," Mr. Aja said. "What do you have in mind?"

"I have a pair of binoculars from the Battle of Gettysburg," Riley said.

"Do you now?" Mr. Aja stopped erasing and turned his full attention to Riley. "They must be, what, almost a hundred and twenty years old. Where did you get something as special as that?"

"They belonged to my father's great-great-grandfather," Riley went on. "He might have fought with a Vermont regiment. My dad got them from his aunt and uncle in Craftsbury. Sam Mitchell told me the Vermonters played a big part in that battle. That's what I'd like to do my research paper on."

"A bona fide hero in your family, eh? I think it's a great idea. Go for it," Mr. Aja said, smiling. "I'll be very interested to see what you come up with. Let me know if I can help."

That's how Riley found himself down in the Sharon Free Library several afternoons each week. He was surprised at the number of books the small library had about the Civil War and Vermont's part in it. The librarian said the Civil War was a favorite topic of Vermonters because they were proud that their small state had been so determined to save the Republic that it had declared war on the South even before Abraham Lincoln had. Some of the books were quite old, and the pages were thin and brittle, like onion skin. When he turned them, the pages clung to each other until he peeled them apart. The library was chilly, and he asked the librarian, who sat at a small desk in the corner, huddled in several sweaters, if he could take the books home, but she said that the books he was using were on the reference shelf and were part of a collection considered so important by everyone in Sharon that no one was allowed to check them out.

He spent hours poring over lists of names of Vermont men who had taken their long slim rifles down off the walls of their homes and gone south to fight for the Union. He read every name in every roster, although the work nearly put him to sleep, hoping to find Silas Griffin's name among them, but he was disappointed.

One afternoon the librarian crept up at his elbow carrying a small, dog-eared box.

"I've been saving these," she confessed.

Riley looked up from another long list and tried to focus his eyes on her. He waited.

"Here are three letters," she said. She put the box down on the corner of the massive oak library table and lifted the lid. "I didn't mention them before because I needed to know that you would take care of them before I entrusted them to you. I think you will, and so I am going to let you have a peek at them." She reached into the box and removed a small package tied with a faded maroon ribbon.

Riley reached for it eagerly.

"Uh-uh!" the librarian remonstrated, pulling the pack-

age back out of his reach. "Gently. These are the only letters Sharon still has from the Civil War. They were written by a man named James Jennison to his wife. And we
have only the three."

"I'll be very, very careful," Riley promised.

He pulled on the ribbon that held the letters together
and the knot unslipped as though it had been tied yes-
terday. The letters were each in their own envelope, a
fragile folding of dingy white paper that threatened to
disintegrate in his hands, all addressed to Sarah Jennison,
Sharon, Vermont. When he removed the letters and tried
to flatten them, the folds groaned as if they were an old
joint locked too long in one position. In the end, he read
the letters still partially folded, afraid that if he persisted
in flattening the paper it would turn to dust in his hands.

Springbreak, Virginia
February 1863

My dear Sarah,

*I writ to tell you that I am now waring the best suit of
cloths I ever wore. I look rit smart and think you wood like
what you see. I have been assined to Vermont's 16 witch
is fine by me because some of the other Sharon boys are
with me.*

yr everloving husband,
James

outside Gettisburg, Penn.

July 1, 1863

Dearest Sarah,

We have been on a long march all day triing to get into pozition to fight tomorrow. I write tonite by campfire. I am almost too tired to lift my pen. We have been told that tomorrow's will be a great battle, posibly desiding the war. I cannot tell you that I am not afrade, but there is no other kourse but this one for good men to follow. The confederates are nothing but scoundrels, cowards who would rather destroy the union than admit that every one of God's creatures has a rightful place upon the Earth. I say my prayers every night, but I wood be gratful if you wood pray for me to.

Love, your husband,

James

Baltimore

July 1863

Oh Sarah, how I miss you. This war has gone on too long and I am a brokn man bekaus of what I have seen and dun. How I long to see my farm in the Vermont hills, to eat an apple from the tree in the front yard and drink milk fresh from the cow. But as the Lord led the children

of Israel, we cannot quit until we have chased these cow-
ardly butternuts from every battlefield. People who are so
wrongheaded in their noshuns must not be allowed to
win or heaven help us all. I think of you every nite and
keep your picshure in my breastpocket, close to my heart.

God willing, I will be home soon. I am, always,

yr loving husband,

James

One day, when Riley had almost finished reading everything the Sharon Free Library had on Vermont in the Civil
War, he took his binoculars down to show them to the
librarian.

"Oh!" she exclaimed, clapping her hands together.
"Whose did you say these were?"

"My great-great-great-grandfather's. That's whose name
I've been looking for in the rosters," he told her. "I didn't
find him, but you said that you didn't have all the lists here."

"That's right," she agreed. "There's many a man who has
not yet gotten credit in our collection. It's a work-in-
progress."

She handled the binoculars gently, rubbing her hand
over their pitted, black paint just the way Sam and Riley
had, as if these old eyepieces were a genie's bottle whose
hero could be released by a soft caress.

"They would be a wonderful addition to the historical society's museum, if we ever have one," she added.

Riley agreed that it would be nice for the historical society to own a pair of binoculars like these so everyone could appreciate a real, live artifact of the Civil War, but he knew he could never give up this pair. He had come to see the Civil War through them. When he put them to his eyes, even up in the solitude of his bedroom, he could see the green and blue colors of the 16th Vermont rippling in the breeze, and beyond them the desperate Confederates coming up the long hot slope of Cemetery Ridge. Then slowly a line of Yankees would pivot into view from the left to mow the foolish butternuts down, a line composed of the Vermont 16th, brave and heroic men like James Jennison and Riley's great-great-great-grandfather, men who were victorious because they had God and right on their side, not to mention all the children of Israel.

✄ ✄ ✄

Sam apologized again that afternoon. It was the second week in March, and he, Riley, and Riley's mother were knee deep in wet snow that grabbed hold of Riley's boots and threatened to pull them off with every step. For all they could see or hear in the sugarbush several hundred yards behind Sam's cabin, they might have been the only people on the planet.

"It's okay," Riley said once more, this time with obvious irritation. He knew Sam was apologizing again for the debacle over the Pledge of Allegiance.

The evening after the incident with Mr. St. Francis, Sam had rushed to the Griffins' house. The pain on his face as he said how sorry he was that his problems had hurt Riley was as real as the fingers on Riley's hand. His mother had looked at Riley, her eyebrows raised in question, but Riley had shaken his head. He hadn't told Sam; he hadn't breathed a word to anyone, but as his mother always said, the truth crawls, gossip flies.

The whole spectacle at the gymnasium was almost six weeks old now, but it still embarrassed Riley, and he wanted to forget everything about it. Looking back on it, he was ashamed of how quickly he had given up the flag, how weak he had looked in front of all those people who were still forming their opinion of him, when he caved in and gave the flag to Mr. Stewart without even making an attempt to stand up for himself. After a few days he had realized that Tim Ferris was the only one who might be tempted to snigger behind his back, but Riley had given him several hard looks that Tim was smart enough to consider warnings.

Now Riley looked at the sled twenty yards away and wondered if he could make it that far. As promised, Sam had invited Riley and his mother to come collect sap with him for boiling down into maple syrup, but Riley was convinced Sam's real name was Tom Sawyer and this was all a clever ploy to avoid the hardest work. Riley and his mother were slogging their way through the deep snow from tree to tree, pouring the pale sap that dripped from metal taps into big buckets and lugging the buckets to the sled. Sam dragged the sled back and forth to the sugarhouse where a blazing wood fire kept the sap bubbling away until it was reduced to amber syrup. The things he was learning living here, he thought. His friends back home probably thought maple syrup came from plastic bottles. If they only knew.

His back ached, his hand ached where the handles cut into his fingers, his legs ached from battling the wet snow. His feet were soaked, his fingers so cold and wet they felt like ice cubes. He was ready to quit, but Sam said they needed to collect from all the trees. Every day for a week. Sap sitting too long in a bucket goes bad, he had explained. So here was Riley after school, out in the woods with his mother, regretting that he had ever expressed to Sam any interest in making syrup.

"What did you find out about Gettysburg and Silas Griffin?" his mother asked as the light in the woods was fading from yellow to blue. He knew she was trying to keep him going through the last stretch. She looks as tired as I feel, Riley thought.

"Lots of stuff," he said. "Vermont lost more soldiers in proportion to its population than any other state."

"It did?" Mrs. Griffin asked in surprise as she lifted a bucket of sap from one tree and poured it into the bucket Riley was holding. "Why?"

"Maybe they wanted to win more than anybody else," Riley said. He guessed that the sap his mother had just added to his bucket must weigh a hundred pounds. At least, that's how it felt. "They wanted to save the country. They thought what the South was doing was wrong."

"What else have you found out about Vermont?"

"That the Battle of Gettysburg was just about the most important battle of the war and the Vermonters were just about the most important soldiers there," Riley said.

"I've heard that before," Sam said, meeting them at the sled to gather buckets. "But I've never known what they did."

"It was the 13th and 16th regiments, mostly," Riley explained. "When Pickett's Charge came up Cemetery Ridge, the Vermonters swung around on the edge like a big door." He held his hands flat up in the air as if they were a shelf, and then swung the fingers of one hand toward the sky to demonstrate. "While the rest of the Union soldiers were shooting at the Rebs face on, the Vermonters shot at them from the side. They could take out a bunch of men with a single bullet that passed down the line. The Rebs couldn't take the fire from both sides, so they chickened out and ran."

"That sounds positively dreadful," his mother said, and shuddered, probably as much from the damp cold as from the gory image of all those bodies, Riley thought.

Sam was silent.

"It was," Riley agreed, wrinkling his nose just at the thought of it. He took off his mitten and rubbed his right hand where it ached. "There are really gross stories about how the doctors cut off legs and arms and just piled them outside the hospital tents. There were fifty thousand casualties at Gettysburg in three days."

"I don't want to hear about the rest. It's too awful, it's too sad," his mother said, zipping her parka up to her chin against the growing chill. "But you would have told us if you'd found Silas Griffin's name anywhere, wouldn't you?"

"I keep looking at all the rosters. Those are the lists of men who fought in each unit," Riley explained, proud of what he had picked up during his hours at the Sharon Free Library. "I haven't found it yet, but there may be more rosters somewhere else. He had to have been there. Almost all the Vermonters were. Everyone says they saved the day, they were the heroes."

"Why?" Sam interrupted quietly. "Because they won the battle? Because they could kill more effectively than the other side?"

✖ *Chapter* THIRTEEN

Slam. Slam. Dunk.

Sam drove into the basket and curled like a cat about to spring. Then there he was, stretched out to his full height, sailing off his feet toward the rim. Dunk.

He bounced the ball to Riley. "Look up," Sam urged. "Trust the ball to find your hand. Keep your eye on the basket."

Riley tried it. The ball bounced twice into his palm and then missed it.

"That's okay," Sam reassured him. "Glance down, find it, and look to the basket again."

Bounce, bounce, bounce. Riley felt as if he were dribbling in slow motion. Finally, the basket came within striking distance. He stopped and crouched and lifted the ball into the air with one hand, just the way Sam had shown him. The ball hit the rim and tottered there, spinning for what seemed like a full minute, and then fell through the net with a whisper.

"Atta way," Sam said, one of his rare smiles lighting his face. He caught the rebound and dribbled back toward the end of the short driveway. "What are your plans for spring vacation?"

"I don't know," Riley said, waiting to see Sam loft the ball effortlessly into the air.

"Look around," Sam said. He shot. The ball arched into the gray sky and slipped through the net without touching the rim.

Riley looked. Snowbanks still lined the driveway. It was early April. The clouds were endless and leaden, like a weight that would never lift. In the few places where the grass peeked through, the earth looked drowned and muddy.

"Let's go south," Sam said. "After you give your presentation in class this week on the Vermont brigades, I propose that we all go to Gettysburg for your school vacation. It's three hundred miles south of here. It will be warmer and greener there. It will feel like spring. It would be good for your mother to see something pretty."

Sam made the same proposal inside the house to Riley's mother, and to Riley's amazement and wonder, she agreed. She said she would arrange to get the time off from work, and she did. But the night before they were to leave, she came down with a fever. In the morning, she could barely talk.

"Go without me," she croaked. She was standing in the doorway of the kitchen, her eyes and cheeks bright with fever.

"We'll wait," Riley said, trying to hide his disappointment.

"No, don't," she insisted. "I'll be fine, but not in time to make the trip. If you don't go now, you won't go at all."

In the end, Riley and Sam piled into Sam's truck. They had been planning on taking the Griffins' car, which seemed to be more securely put together, but Sam wanted to leave it behind for Riley's mother in case she needed it.

Sam patted the dashboard.

"Let's hope for the best," he said.

They had egg salad sandwiches in a cooler behind the seat and Silas Griffin's binoculars wrapped in a towel on Riley's lap. He liked the feel of them there, the round hard cylinders of the eyepieces that fit his hands so well, even through the padding.

"I hope you find him," Riley's mother called from the back porch, where she was shivering in her red bathrobe. She blew them both another kiss, and Riley looked the other way so Sam wouldn't see him blushing.

It was nearly seven hours to Gettysburg, but spring was more apparent with every passing mile. First the snow disappeared, then the grass turned the breathless green of emeralds, then the daffodils exploded into bloom, their yellow heads nodding as the truck passed by, then the trees wore halos of red buds, and finally, leaves emerged in a hundred shades of spring green.

They pulled into Gettysburg at twilight and found a room at a cheap motel on the outskirts of town.

"Can we go look?" Riley asked.

"That's what we came for," Sam said.

Weary though they were, they climbed back into the truck and drove into Gettysburg National Military Park. It was nearly empty at that hour, all the visitors' information centers were closed, and they had the roads almost to themselves.

"It's bigger than I imagined," Riley said as they passed the silent green fields and followed one of the roads into the woods. "I thought it would look different. I thought everything would be close together, that you would be able to see what was going on wherever you were."

"It looks like many men wouldn't have had a clue what was going on except where they were fighting," Sam said. Darkness was falling fast. "Let's not do it all tonight. That would spoil it. We'll come back in the morning, bright and early, and spend the day."

� ✗ ✗

The morning was cool. A curtain of clouds covered the sky, but it was thin enough to make the sky bright. By the time Sam and Riley arrived at the park, the lot was already filling with cars and campers bearing license plates from all over the United States.

"Look at that," Riley marveled. "There are people here from everywhere."

When they worked their way inside the visitors' center, a crowd four people thick was milling around in front of the information desk.

"Let's come back later. I know you want to get going," Sam said. "We'll just grab a few brochures and do it ourselves today. We have all day tomorrow, too."

They started next door in a building with a cavernous room where a simulated battlefield was laid out on the floor like a giant model train set. While a man's deep voice narrated the events of the first four days of July 1863, little lights planted in the set lit up to show the tourists which regiments were arriving from which direction and where the troops were taking up their stations.

"It was huge," Riley said in awe, watching the hundreds of lights shift and sweep across the model as regiments took up new positions and the battles shifted ground.

Afterward, Sam and Riley took off in the truck with a map. They didn't miss anything: Little Round Top, Devil's Den, the wheatfield, Culp's Hill, the Peach Orchard, Seminary Ridge. Riley was familiar with the grand landscape of the battle and skirmish sites from his long winter afternoons in the library, but seeing them in person was different.

After months of looking up at Vermont's hills and mountains, Riley stood at the crest of Little Round Top, looking down over the greening Pennsylvania countryside, and complained, "This isn't anything more than a bump."

"That may be true," Sam agreed, "but if it's nearly the highest thing around, I guess it gives you an advantage over everyone else."

They saved Cemetery Ridge for last. They pulled up and parked near the clump of trees that had been the center of the Union defense. Stretching before them was a shallow valley, one mile wide, covered in farm fields. A mile to the west were the woods along Seminary Ridge. A flock of sparrows blew up the slight incline and wheeled away to the left as fluid as running water. Occasionally, they could hear a car moving along the Emmitsburg Road, but not even the slight breeze teasing the young spring leaves disturbed the peace.

"This is where Pickett's Charge was," Riley told Sam. He reached over the seat and pulled the binoculars out of his backpack before he climbed out of the truck. Standing on the new grass, he carefully put the worn strap over his head, took off his glasses, and brought the binoculars up to his eyes. Just as Sam had said, the old glass made the scene before his eyes different from anything he had imagined. The line of distant, indistinct trees came into focus. Riley could see the green crowns of century-old trees, the individual brown trunks lined up like troops, and underbrush like the bushes that had once shielded thousands of Rebel soldiers from the scrutiny of Union sharpshooters standing where Riley now stood and ready to blow off their heads.

"It's hard to believe," Sam said, coming around the front of the truck to join him.

"What?" Riley asked. With the glasses pressed to his nose, he continued to sweep the fields and woods.

"It's so beautiful now, so peaceful and still," Sam said softly. A few birds called to each other. "It's impossible for me to imagine what happened here."

Sam reached into the truck and plucked one of the brochures off the seat. "Listen to what one of the Union soldiers said he saw: 'An overwhelming resistless tide of an ocean of armed men sweeping upon us! . . . on they move, as with one soul, in perfect order . . . over ridge and slope, through orchard and meadow and cornfield, magnificent, grim, irresistible.'"

"They weren't so irresistible," Riley said. "The Vermonters got 'em."

"Not alone," Sam reminded him.

"No," Riley admitted, "but they helped save the day. And Silas Griffin was probably one of them."

When they finally returned to the visitors' center, the afternoon was fading. The crowds had thinned. Riley stretched out on a bench while Sam went over to speak to one of the park guides. He came back fifteen minutes later with more brochures and pamphlets in his hand.

"Riley," he said, "come with me."

"Why? Where are we going?" Riley asked as he tagged along behind.

"I just found out where the library is. We can find out what regiment Silas Griffin was in, and where he fought," Sam said, his long legs striding toward a round building sitting on a knoll several hundred yards away.

As Riley and Sam stepped through the doorway into the park's narrow library, a middle-aged man wearing a green and tan park uniform said, "I'm one of the park historians. May I help you?" For a second they didn't answer, so overwhelming was the volume of information that apparently lay before them in the thousands of books squeezed into the rows of bookshelves that stretched across the room.

"We're looking for someone," Sam replied after gathering his wits.

"Oh?" the man asked. He turned to look at the scattering of people hunched over their books and papers at the worktables. Other staff, also in uniform, were wandering around carrying books and leaning over shoulders speaking softly. "Do you see him or her?"

"No," Riley explained. His heart was beating faster, and he found himself getting excited. "He means we want to find out something about someone who fought at Gettysburg. My great-great-great-grandfather."

"In that case," the man said with satisfaction, "I can help you after all. Do you have a name?"

"Silas Griffin," Riley volunteered.

"Do you know what regiment he fought for?"

"No," Riley admitted. "But it was from Vermont."

"Vermont?" the historian asked. "Are you sure?"

"No," Sam said. "We think it might have been Vermont."

"Well, without knowing what regiment he was in, or even what state he was from, it's difficult to find a name." The park historian turned from them and looked out across the sea of tables and books. "We have thousands of names here. Tens of thousands. I'm sure you understand."

"But we came all the way from Vermont to find out," Riley protested. He looked at Sam pleadingly.

"What did you say your great-great-great-grandfather's name was?" the man asked. "Did you say his first name was Silas?"

"Yes," Riley said firmly. "Silas Griffin."

"Then wait here. Perhaps there is some hope," he said, and walked away. He was gone for a full two minutes, and when he reappeared from the stacks he was leading an elderly man by the elbow. Eventually, the two park historians parted ways, and the old man made his way alone toward Riley and Sam. He walked stiffly, and his park uniform hung loosely on him, as if underneath it was the skeleton of a bird. Watching him approach with an air of quiet dignity, Riley thought there was something wrong with him, but it was clear as the man came close that it was merely age. His head was fringed with wispy white hair, and flakes from his face and scalp littered his tan shirt.

"Mr. Emery thinks I might be of some assistance," he said as he came to a stop in front of them. "I hope so. My name is Mr. Hoyt. How do you do?"

He stuck out a frail, white hand and limply shook hands, first with Sam and then with Riley.

"I understand the Christian name of the soldier in question is Silas," Mr. Hoyt said. "Is that correct?"

"Yes," Riley answered, although he was confused by what the Christian part meant.

"And what is the surname?" Mr. Hoyt asked. When Riley looked baffled, he added, "His last name, young man. Your surname is your last name, your family name."

"Griffin," Riley said. "His name was Silas Griffin. He was from Vermont."

"This is really rather extraordinary." Mr. Hoyt smiled a small smile. "But I believe I have come across that name."

Riley was shocked.

"You mean you know everybody's name? Everyone who fought here?" Riley could hardly believe this.

"No, not at all." Mr. Hoyt chuckled. "Although it *is* true that most of us who work here have become familiar over the years with many of the names. We have looked at thousands of them, but we are trained to have sharp memories. Having a good memory saves a great deal of time and trouble in the searches." He slowly raised his right hand and tapped his temple.

"But you remember Silas Griffin?" Riley asked, still disbelieving.

"My great-grandfather's name was also Silas," the man explained. "It was not a rare name back then, but it was uncommon enough that over the years I've kept an eye out for it in the rosters. In fact, I have kept a short list in a notebook of the Silases I have found. Just as a hobby, you understand. I believe I know where we can find Silas Griffin's name. Incidentally, young man, you were close; it's a 'V': But he was a Virginian, not a Vermonter. Please follow me."

"He couldn't have been a Virginian," Riley protested as he followed on the elderly man's heels.

"We'll see if I've made a mistake. I do sometimes, you know." Mr. Hoyt smiled down at Riley. "Have a seat. I will bring you the regimental rosters."

Sam and Riley sat at a long table and waited.

"He must be wrong," Riley insisted.

"Let's take a look," Sam said.

The search took almost no time at all. After the hours Riley had spent reading those endless rosters of Vermont names in the Sharon Free Library, looking in vain for Silas Griffin's name, the elderly park historian laid the roster in front of Riley and Sam and opened it almost at once to the page that was headed *Fourteenth Virginia Regiment. Commander, General Lewis Armistead.* Underneath was a long, unbroken list of names, listed alphabetically. Halfway down the page, Riley found what he was looking for: *Griffin, Silas. Residence, Palmyra. Date of Enlistment, October 10, 1862. Date of muster, October 12, 1862. Died July 3, 1863.*

"If he was in one of Armistead's regiments, and he died on July third, he died in Pickett's Charge," Mr. Hoyt said, trying to be helpful.

Riley stared at the page, speechless.

"I don't get it," he said finally.

"There must be more than one Silas Griffin," Sam insisted, as if he was also having trouble believing what he saw.

"Perhaps," Mr. Hoyt admitted. "However, I do not recall ever seeing that name in the Vermont rosters. Have you ever found his name listed in a Vermont roster?"

"No." Riley's voice was barely a whisper.

"It is very likely, then, that this is your great-great-great-grandfather," Mr. Hoyt said. "As I mentioned earlier, Silas was a rather uncommon name."

How could this be? Riley's mind raced. Silas Griffin was a Virginian who fought for the Confederacy. He didn't save anything. He died at Gettysburg on July 3, 1863, trying to break the Union in half.

"You did this!" Riley dumped his chair over backward and turned on Sam, shouting even as everyone in the library turned to gape at them. Mr. Hoyt's face turned even whiter, and he took a step backward. "This is all your fault! You ruined this! I never, ever asked to come here. This was all your dumb idea!"

"Riley, I'm sorry," Sam stammered. He tried to rise, but his chair and the table held him. Awkwardly, he raised his big prayer hands palms outward in front of his chest. "I had no idea."

"Silas Griffin was my great-great-great-grandfather! He was *my* hero!" Riley yelled. "He belonged to me! I've lost everything I've ever had. My dad, Cassie, Stony Point, my home, my friends, and now this! You told me Silas Griffin was a hero!"

"I didn't," Sam protested. "I told you the Vermonters played an important part."

"Well, Silas Griffin wasn't one of them!" Riley shouted. "He fought for the other side! He was a loser, just like you."

Riley turned and bolted. He pushed past a woman at the door and nearly knocked her over, but he didn't stop, not even after she shouted, "Excuse you!" at his back. He ran from the library and across the lawn into the vast fields and woods of the park. He ran until his chest heaved and his side throbbed, and he had no idea where he was before he collapsed in the damp grass.

He lay on his back, the great purple dome of the sky a blur, the tears streaming from his eyes into his ears, while he pounded the ground with his fists. He cried until he was hoarse, until he became aware of the stubble under his shoulders and the chilly dew soaking his shirt.

When he finally sat up, it was almost dark. The moon had not yet risen, but a few stars glittered overhead. He could tell it was long past supper because his stomach felt empty. The park was quiet, deathly quiet, as quiet as a place can be more than one hundred years after thousands of men died there, and Riley held his breath as he grew aware of where he was and what had happened here. He could suddenly feel the hair on the back of his neck straighten.

He stumbled out onto the road, vaguely remembering his way, not from his angry and disappointed escape in the late afternoon, which was just a blur, but from his ride in Sam's truck that morning. It must have been more than a mile along that black ribbon of asphalt to the park entrance. Riley ran, a long, dark, terrifying run through the battlefield's unfamiliar territory, past lone trees with their looming black shadows, past woods that crowded the road and hid heaven knew what, past marble statues of soldiers rising from the damp earth like ghosts, past open fields that made him feel exposed and alone. All he could think about was running and the whine of a bullet coming out of nowhere and thwacking into the tree beside his head and the bones that might still be decaying in the ground under his feet. That thought made him gag, and he tried to run on his toes to touch the ground as little as possible. When he finally saw the lights of the town, he almost started crying again, but he had a painful cramp in his side and no breath left.

Out in the bustle of the main street, he was lucky. He started walking alongside the busy road, but someone soon offered him a ride and he was weary enough to accept it in spite of all his mother's warnings about accepting rides from strangers. He got out at the edge of town, just fifty yards from the motel. Sam's beat-up truck was parked in front of their unit.

Sam opened the door the minute Riley knocked. His eyes were sunken and almost black, and his thick hair stood out in disarray.

"I'll call the park police and tell them you're here. I just came back to call your mother and tell her I'd lost you," Sam said.

Riley walked past him without saying anything and went into the bathroom to wash his face.

When he came out, he said, "I'm hungry."

"There's a sandwich and a soda for you near the phone," Sam said.

Riley ate it while Sam watched him.

"I'm sorry, Riley," he said. "You know this isn't the way I expected it to turn out."

"I'm going to bed," Riley said. "I want to go home in the morning."

"We can't," Sam said.

"Why not?"

"I've already hired a guide to take us through the park in the morning. I made the reservation when I went into the visitors' center this afternoon. I wanted it to be a surprise," Sam said.

"I won't go," Riley said. "You go if you want to."

"I think you should," Sam urged. "I think you should learn what you came here to learn. Besides, it was expensive and I've already paid for it. It takes two hours. The guide comes along in your car."

"I've already learned more than I wanted to," Riley said.

"All the same, we've come this far, I think you should go," Sam said.

"Suit yourself," Riley said. "You've said it yourself. Fair is fair. I'll go on the tour, but I don't promise I'm going to listen. Then we'll go home."

"Fair is fair," Sam said. "We'll leave as soon as it's over."

❧ ❧ ❧

At nine they arrived at the visitors' center, where the tours started. Riley stayed in the truck. Sam disappeared and returned a few minutes later with a middle-aged woman with curly brown hair. Like all the other staff, she was wearing a green and tan park uniform, and dark, clunky shoes no girls would be caught dead in at school.

"I'm Pat," she said, sticking out her hand to Riley. He reached through the window and extended a limp hand, but he didn't say a word.

"Would you like to sit by the window?" she asked him.

Grudgingly, Riley stepped down and let Pat slide into the middle of the seat. He climbed in last and slouched against the door. Sam started the engine, and Pat directed them down the road.

As much as he could, Riley ignored everything Pat had to say. She talked, and Sam asked questions, but Riley stared out the window deaf and blind to whatever they talked about or pointed to.

Once, in spite of himself, when Pat was talking about the Confederates trying to take Little Round Top while the Union soldiers defended that precious vantage point, all of the fighting taking place in woods so dense that no one could see beyond a couple of dozen yards, Riley remembered last night when he had been stumbling in the dark, unsure of where he was, his heart pounding in his chest like a jackhammer.

When they must have covered just about everything there was to see, Pat told Sam to pull off the road. Riley came out of his sulk long enough to glance at his watch. The tour was nearly over.

"Let's get out," Pat said.

Sam opened his door and stepped down, and Riley assumed that Pat would slide out Sam's door, but she waited for Riley. Reluctantly, he opened his door and put his feet on the ground. Pat landed beside him.

"That's Seminary Ridge," she said, pointing to a line of trees a mile away, "where Pickett's men lined up, nearly twelve thousand of them, to make their charge. This is Cemetery Ridge." She pointed to the small copse of trees nearby and the intersection of a pair of stone walls, neither of them higher than Riley's waist. "That's the Angle. That marked the center of the Union position.

"What state did you say you were from?" she asked, turning to Riley.

"Vermont," he said, although he knew as well as she did that she had never asked for that information before, and he had never given it. She was trying to get his attention. Go ahead and try, he said to himself.

"Oh, well, you probably know the Vermont regiments helped carry the day here on July third," she said. She took a few steps forward and pointed. "See that statue with the soldier on top? That's the Vermont monument, marking where the Vermonters fought that day. When they swung around here on a pivot," she said, swinging her arm like a door on a hinge, "the Vermonters had clear shots down the whole of the Confederate line. The Southerners couldn't possibly fight on two fronts at once.

"I often wonder," she continued, "how the Confederates ever found the courage to step out in the first place. After the war, one of the Union commanders said that when all twelve thousand Southern soldiers stepped out together in a long line, it was one of the most beautiful things he had ever seen. But it must have been a terrible beauty. Look at that exposure. It's remarkable. They had to cover more than a mile of open ground to gain this ridge. And all the while, the Union troops were bombarding them with their cannons, hiding behind these stone walls, and firing on them mercilessly." Her arm swept over the landscape, taking in the fields, the old fences, and the woods far beyond. "Close to eight thousand of them died or were captured trying to take the spot you're standing on, and nearly every one of them feared he was doomed when he took his first step. General Lee said afterward, 'This has all been my fault.' It was an unspeakable tragedy, and it must have been a terrible burden for him to bear."

"Why did he do it?" Riley blurted out in spite of himself. "Why did any of them do it? It was so stupid! Look at it! How could they walk right into those bullets if they knew they were going to die, if they knew they were going to lose?"

"That's a hard question to answer without asking them," Pat said. "They were very brave men. I don't think they were necessarily thinking so much about what they might lose as about what might be gained if, by the grace of God, they succeeded. They very possibly would have won the war if they had been victorious here. They were certainly misguided about the Negroes, but for most of the war, the Southerners fought on their own land to protect the only way of life they knew. They had a sense of something great being at stake."

"But they lost!" Riley cried out, as if any of them could forget that, standing there in the bright sun behind the stone walls where the Northern troops had found shelter.

Pat pulled her eyes away from the panorama before them and looked at Riley.

"Win or lose, it sometimes takes tremendous courage to stand up for your principles," she said. "You can never take that away from them."

✴ *Chapter* FOURTEEN

They drove for an hour, pressing northward up through the Delaware Water Gap, where skunk cabbage sprouted and bloomed beside the road and the new leaves of the trees fluttered like a million flags. Sam's truck did the only talking, sputtering and coughing like an old man, and finally dying altogether.

Sam struggled to coax the truck onto the shoulder of the road. As soon as it had drifted to a stop, he slammed both his hands down so hard on the steering wheel that Riley jumped.

"Damn!" he said. He turned to Riley, his dark eyes burning with frustration and disappointment. "I can't tell you how sorry I am about all of this. The whole trip has been a disaster. I'm sorry I ever brought it up."

Then he climbed out and lifted the hood. Riley didn't move, didn't make one effort to help as he listened to Sam moving around the engine, tinkering with the ancient parts. Finally, Sam slammed the hood down and climbed back in.

"Let's see if that will do it," he said more calmly.

The engine sputtered and caught when he turned the key.

"Okay," Sam said. He breathed a deep, shuddering sigh of relief. "We're back on the road. But we're going to have to take it slow."

"Why don't you just get a new truck?" Riley complained, glad to have something else to pick on Sam for.

"I can't afford it," Sam replied, as if he hadn't noticed Riley's tone. "I probably can't even afford a new *used* truck."

"You work!" Riley insisted as other cars sped past them. It was a statement of fact, but he made it sound like an accusation, and he wasn't sorry about that either.

"I do," Sam said, "but it's pretty much hand-to-mouth living. It's hard to make much money doing carpentry in a town like Sharon."

"Then move! Get a real job, for Pete's sake!" Riley threw his hands up in the air. The solution was so obvious to him.

"It's not that simple," Sam said. He turned and looked sidewise at Riley. "How much do you know about me?"

"Enough," Riley said.

"You know I was drafted and sent to Vietnam?" Sam asked.

"Everybody knows that," Riley snorted.

"And you've heard that I refused to fight," Sam said.

"Everybody knows that, too," Riley said.

"Do you know why?" Sam asked.

"You just wouldn't fight," Riley said. "That's what everybody says." He left out the part about how a number of people thought Sam was an outright coward with a yellow stripe a mile wide down his back.

They drove on in silence for a while. The sky had grown dark, and metal-gray rain clouds began scudding across the sky. In the trees alongside the road, the new green leaves flipped up, as they do before a storm, and their pale undersides flickered silver as the wind played among the branches. Raindrops began to splatter on the windshield.

"It's true I don't believe in killing. Cows or deer or men. But I think I would have enlisted for the Union in the Civil War," Sam said. "I could have justified it. I would have fought to save the country. That would have been clear enough and important enough for me."

"Why couldn't you fight in Vietnam?" Riley asked, curious in spite of himself.

"No one ever gave me a reason for that war that made any sense," Sam said. "And I couldn't take a life without knowing why I was killing. So first they threw me in jail, and then they sent me home with a dishonorable discharge."

"I still don't see what that has to do with being a carpenter," Riley said.

"You will someday," Sam said, "when you start filling out college and job applications. On every one of them, there's a line that asks for your military record, including whether you were honorably or dishonorably discharged.

When I tried to go back to college, and later when I went looking for work, every form asked the same question."

Sam turned and looked at Riley.

"I could fill in the word 'honorably,' even though that's not what my discharge papers say, but I'm not a liar. I'm not a coward either, but I'm too ashamed of the word 'dishonorable' and all that it conjures up in people's minds to fill in that word either," he said. "So I've spent my life avoiding that line, that one line. I still think I did the right thing, but I've come to believe that that line is like a ghost that will haunt me the rest of my life. Because of it I never went back to art school and I've never worked for anyone but myself. I've never married, I've never had children. I live in a cabin at the end of a dirt road. I've lived in Sharon all my life except for the year I spent in college and the army, and I think I've been a good citizen, but there are some people who won't speak to me. Sometimes, I wonder if it's all been worth it. Maybe it would have been easier to pick up that gun and start killing."

They rode on for several minutes in silence.

"It tears me apart," Sam began, his voice choked and low. Surprised, Riley turned to look at him, but Sam didn't take his eyes off the wet asphalt ahead. "It makes me feel so guilty to think that Mary St. Francis's life has been made even harder because her father, who was a stupid, insensitive clod of a classmate of mine, went to

Vietnam and did what I was asked to do but couldn't, because I believed, as a matter of principle, that what my country was asking of me was wrong. I don't mind that people think Stanley St. Francis is a hero. What he did took courage. What bothers me is that he went to Vietnam just because his country asked him to go, and he started killing without ever asking what those lives were being taken for."

✄ ✄ ✄

By now the rain was coming down in torrents. The truck's tired windshield wipers slapped noisily and pushed the water around without really moving much of it off the glass. Sam turned on the radio and fiddled with the dial until he found a country music station with a woman wailing about her no-good husband.

A red sports car sped past them on the left, and a blue delivery van came up hard on its tail. In less time than Riley had to blink, the red car started hydroplaning on the rain-slicked road, its rear end sliding around in front of them. Sam slammed on the brakes. The van was too close to the red car for the driver to react. The nose of the red car clipped the right front corner of the van as the car pirouetted on the wet road.

Riley watched in horror as the two vehicles became entangled, their bumpers locked together like ballroom dancers. Together the car and the van waltzed, as if in slow motion, gradually sliding off the road, separating and rolling over and over until they came to rest on their roofs.

Sam stopped the truck and was sprinting over the wet asphalt toward the vehicles in long strides even before Riley's brain had fully taken in what he had just seen.

"Grab the blanket behind the seat!" Sam shouted over his shoulder, oblivious to the rain pelting his back.

Riley fumbled with the soda cans and bags until he could pull the blanket free. His heart was beating so loudly that it left no room for air in his chest. He clutched the blanket in his arms and ran out into the rain toward where the two vehicles lay stranded on their backs like turtles.

The driver of the van was standing numbly in the grassy median. His eyes were unfocused and his mouth was hanging open. He had a small cut above his right ear.

Sam was pulling frantically at the back door of the red car. Inside a little girl was screaming, hanging upside down in her seat belt.

"Riley! Help me!" Sam shouted without looking back.

Riley dropped the blanket and ran without thinking to join Sam in pulling on the door. A thin stream of smoke was beginning to drift upward from the engine. Together they pulled until Riley thought the muscles in his neck would burst, and finally the door began to give. Sam reached through and unbuckled the seat belt, and the little girl fell into his arms.

"Take her!" Sam ordered Riley.

She was no bigger than Claire. She was crying hysterically and had a long cut on her cheek, but she struggled hard in Riley's arms and he doubted she could be seriously hurt. Instinctively, he ducked to shield her from the rain while he ran back toward the damp blanket. Other drivers had stopped, and they formed a half moon of spectators, but no one moved. Riley glanced back and knew why. Flames had begun to lick up through the wheel wells.

Riley could see a woman slumped against the steering wheel. Sam was pulling frantically on the doorknob, but the door wasn't moving. Finally, he grabbed a piece of metal that had been torn loose from one of the vehicles and began pounding on the window. More smoke was curling up from the car, but Sam swung again and again, until the window shattered and fell free in a thousand pieces from the frame. Now Riley could hear the woman sobbing.

"Help me! Oh, God, help me! Don't let me burn!"

In the end, Sam dragged her sobbing out through the window and carried her well away from the car. When the mother saw her child, she screamed and reached for her. Riley could hear sirens wailing in the background now.

Someone volunteered a dry blanket, but by then most of the work had been done. They all watched as the car burst into flames that hissed and sputtered in the falling rain.

The accident held them up for almost an hour and a half. One ambulance carried off the woman and her daughter. Another took the van driver. Both ambulances inched their way from the grassy median back onto the highway and headed south, their sirens crying out for everyone's attention.

A third set of ambulance attendants treated Sam for some small cuts on his hands from the shattered glass. Riley watched as they worked over those long gentle prayer hands, cleaning the wounds and dabbing at them with Mercurochrome. Then Sam and Riley sat in a police car, out of the rain, while Sam gave his report of what he'd seen. Riley had little to add. It had all happened too fast. He hadn't had any time to think about what he'd done; he'd just done what his instincts told him to do, what had felt right.

When Sam and Riley finally got back on the road, Sam said almost immediately, "Let's stop. I need a cup of coffee and we both need to change our clothes. You're soaked. Your mother will never forgive me if I bring you home sick."

They found a truck stop a few miles up the road and pulled off. Riley was ravenous. He ordered a sandwich and two pieces of apple pie. Sam drank two cups of coffee, but refused to eat. His face was drawn and his eyes were weary and lined with red.

Back on the road once more, Sam looked at his watch.

"We're going to be pretty late getting you home," he said. "Your mother's going to worry."

"Do you love my mom?" Riley asked.

"I do," Sam said, "very much." He looked at Riley and smiled a slow, sad smile. "Just between you and me, I always have, ever since high school. I'm pretty fond of you, too."

"Are you going to ask her to marry you?"

"I don't think so," Sam said, shaking his head slowly.

"Why not?" Riley asked. "If you love her. She talks about you all the time."

"I'm not sure that I can ask her," Sam confessed. "It's related to what we were talking about earlier."

"I don't get it," Riley said.

"I still think I did the right thing thirteen years ago. I'll always regret I wasn't more successful, but I was trying to persuade other people that the war was wrong," Sam explained, looking straight ahead now. "Unfortunately, I've had a very hard time learning to accept the consequences and what they've meant to my life. I'm not sure I can ask someone else to accept them, too."

The rain kept falling, but not as hard. Along the roadside, spring turned back to late winter. Here and there, Riley could see snow in the mountains as they left New York State and entered Vermont. He dozed the last hour or two as darkness set in. When they finally reached home, Riley stumbled up the stairs to the back porch, where his mother was waiting.

"Did you find him, honey?" she asked as she hugged him despite his efforts to escape.

"No," he said, too tired and too disappointed to make much protest. "At least, I didn't find what I wanted."

Sam was coming up the steps behind Riley. He didn't say a word.

"What do you mean?" his mother asked. She pushed Riley to arm's length and looked at him in the glow of the porch light.

"Silas Griffin wasn't a Vermonter! He wasn't even a Yankee! He was a Confederate, for crying out loud," Riley cried, his disappointment rising again to the surface. "He was at Pickett's Charge, all right, but he fought for Virginia."

"There's more to it than that," Sam urged him on.

"He died right there, trying to take a stupid stone wall," Riley added. "If you could have seen it, Mom, it wasn't even really a hill. Just a ridge. Hardly anything at all, not even good enough for sledding. Why would anyone die for that?"

"He was willing to fight for that ridge because he believed in his cause. If the Confederates had taken the ridge, it would have meant everything," Sam pressed, looking at Riley. "It would have made all the difference in the world in that battle, maybe even in the whole war."

"Yeah, I guess," Riley admitted. "It sure wasn't worth throwing his life away just for the hill."

✄ ✄ ✄

Upstairs, rummaging through his backpack looking for his toothbrush, he came across the binoculars wrapped in their towel. He took them out and looked at them. He hardly knew what to think as he studied Silas Griffin's name etched into the dull paint and rusting now almost 118 years after his death under the broiling sun on that broad expanse of green grass.

Then he raised them to his eyes and tried to imagine Silas looking through the binoculars up the rise from Seminary Ridge to Cemetery Ridge, where the Union troops were massed and waiting behind that stone wall with their cannons and sharpshooters. He wondered if, in spite of the old glass's imperfections, his great-great-great-grandfather had been able to see the individual branches, each in the full leaf of summer, and the day's scorching heat rising in waves from the hot fields. To his surprise, he was grateful for how merciful it might have been if Silas Griffin had not been able to see too clearly the grim faces of all the Yankee soldiers lying in wait.

He thought about what Pat had said about how much courage it must have taken for Silas to take that first step, knowing what he knew about his chances. And he silently thanked Sam for making him go on the tour. If he hadn't, Riley probably would always have thought that Silas Griffin was a loser, Silas Griffin who had marched directly into the face of death because he thought it was the right thing to do for his country. If he lived to be a hundred, Riley realized with a shudder, he would never forget the deadly thwack of Tim Ferris's bullet burying itself in the tree beside him. And that, he reminded himself, had been just a single shot, not a barrage that stopped all sense of place and time. His face burned again with the memory that he had wet himself in fear.

Even if Silas Griffin had been a Confederate, Riley found himself hoping he had died quickly, of a minié ball through the heart or something like that. He didn't want to think that his great-great-great-grandfather might have been one of the wounded crying on the battlefield after the smoke cleared, only to have his leg sawed off and tossed in a pile before he died.

He put the binoculars with their pitted paint and imperfect glass back in the case Sam had made for them and cleared a place for the case on his dresser. It looked good there, he decided.

He brushed his teeth and climbed into bed. After having been away for two nights, he was startled to see the familiar pattern of orange light from the school glowing through the old glass in his window and illuminating his bedroom. The glass caught the light and bent it into waves as graceful as a bird in flight.

Downstairs he could hear Sam telling his mother about the car crash, although he said very little about his own part and concentrated on explaining how Riley had helped pull the little girl from the car.

Before Riley fell asleep, he thought about what Sam had said in the truck, and what Sam had done, and what it had cost him trying to make a difference, too. He wondered if it was ever less painful to die for what you believed in than to live for it.

ℵ *Chapter* FIFTEEN

Riley had never seen spring come to Stony Point the way it came to Sharon. It was as if, having waited so long, spring could not wait another minute. It exploded, bursting like fireworks across the fields and hills and even the mountaintops in a riot of green.

"I remember telling you that Christmas is the most beautiful time of the year in Sharon," said his mother as he worked beside her in the garden Sam had tilled behind their house a few days earlier. "I may have been wrong. This may be better. When you live here, you certainly wait long enough for it."

She raised her head and inhaled deeply, and Riley laughed because the pungent smell of manure spread on all the nearby fields filled the air. He had not expected springtime in Vermont to smell quite so ripe.

Riley was poking twigs in the ground at the head of furrows and unwinding string along the length of the shallow trenches to mark the straight lines where the seeds would go. In the distance he could hear the rumble of a tractor as one of the neighboring farmers plowed a field of dark earth to ready it for planting.

"Can we grow pumpkins?" Riley asked. He felt silly asking. He would be thirteen in a few weeks, and he felt that perhaps he was beyond the age of pumpkins. But he had never had a garden before, and he was curious to see how their work today would bear fruit in a couple of months.

"They need a lot of room," his mother said, looking around. "They grow with what you would call 'wild abandon,' but I don't see why not. Let's give them that far corner. I've never grown pumpkins before either, not even as a child. Let's see what happens."

The first weekend in May was still early for planting most things, but Sam had said that peas, spinach, and radishes could be safely planted even though the danger of frost was not yet past. Riley wondered why there was any rush to plant those particular vegetables. Among all the vegetables his mother talked of planting in this garden, those three would be the ones Riley most hoped would succumb to a cold night.

Neither Riley nor his mother heard Mary until she spoke. Their heads snapped up.

"Excuse me," Mary said politely. She was holding Claire's hand. Both of them were dressed in mismatched outfits, part corduroy, part plaid flannel, part cotton.

"Hi," Riley said with surprise. He stood up and wiped his dirty hands on his jeans. His mother stood up, too.

"I don't believe we've ever officially met," his mother

said. She wiped her hand on her pants and extended it. "I'm Kate Griffin. You're Mary St. Francis, aren't you?"

"Yes, ma'am. How do you do," Mary said, taking her hand. "This is my little sister, Claire."

"Hello, Claire. It's nice to meet you, too," Riley's mother said. She stuck her hand out again, but Claire lowered her eyes and stepped behind Mary.

An awkward silence followed.

Claire spoke first. "I'm thiwsty," she said in a little voice that sounded as if it belonged to a doll.

"Well, come with me. We'll see what we can do about that," Riley's mother said. She held out her hand to Claire, and this time the little girl took it. The two of them walked off toward the back porch.

"It seemed like a good afternoon not to be at my house," Mary explained. "I started out to take Claire to the playground, but once we got there, I wondered, if you were free, you might want to play chess. The state tournament is in two weeks."

Riley looked at the garden and then at his dirty hands.

"It's not a good time," Mary said.

"No, really, it's a great time. My mother is talking about planting peas and spinach."

They both laughed.

"Maybe if we're lucky, they won't come up," Riley added. "Let me wash my hands and get my set. Come on in." He led the way up the porch and into the kitchen.

"Is it okay if we play chess, Mom?" Riley asked. His mother was sitting at the kitchen table with Claire and two glasses of lemonade.

"That's fine with me," said his mother. "Mary, would you like some lemonade?"

"No, thank you," Mary answered.

"Well, then, Claire," Mrs. Griffin said, "that leaves you and me. Would you like to help me finish up in the garden?"

Claire nodded solemnly.

Riley brought his chess pieces and Sam's board down to the porch, but it was still too cool to sit in the shade, so they moved out onto the grass in the bright yellow sunshine. They could hear the murmur of Claire and Riley's mother talking as they worked in the garden, and finally Riley and Mary heard the porch door slam as the two of them went into the house.

Pawn. Pawn. Pawn. Knight. Pawn. Rook. Bishop. Check. Checkmate.

Pawn. Pawn. Knight. Bishop. Rook. Queen. Castle the king. Checkmate.

Pawn. Pawn. Pawn. Pawn. Bishop. Knight. Rook. Queen. Checkmate.

Riley won every game. He could see Mary growing first frustrated and then discouraged. He started taking less time with his moves, thinking he might get careless, create an opening for her to find an advantage, but it didn't work.

"You're not trying anymore," she accused him finally.

"That's not true," he said, but there was an element of truth to it. He wasn't trying very hard now; he wanted her to win. He was not taking the best moves he could think of.

Even before Riley had won, Mary laid her king on its side.

"This is stupid," she said hotly. "You're a better player than I am. You should be going to the tournament, not me. I'll only lose. Plus you have the most beautiful board in the world. I think it's good luck. For you, not me."

She brushed her long hair back over her shoulders and sighed.

"Let's do something else," Riley suggested. "We could shoot baskets. We could take Claire over to the swings."

Mary looked at the position of the sun.

"We should probably be going home," she said. "It's getting close to time to start supper."

Riley thought about asking his mother if Mary and Claire could stay for whatever meatless concoction his mother was inventing tonight, but he didn't know how to bring it up. Besides, he wondered, if Mary doesn't make supper at her house, who would?

When they went in the house, Riley's mother was chopping onions. Riley recognized the smell of brown rice cooking. Claire was sitting at the kitchen table with construction paper, tape, scissors, and Riley's paper chain.

"I was looking for something for Claire to work on," Mrs. Griffin explained. "Then I remembered this chain. You don't seem to have touched it since you rehung it after Christmas. I hope it's okay if Claire is adding links to it."

Riley gave a wave of his hand. "She can have it. I'm done with it," he said.

"Weally?" Claire asked. "It's gigantic!" Her brown eyes danced with delight.

Mary walked over to the refrigerator, where Riley's mother had taped the small article that had been in the *Sharon Courier* reporting Sam's and Riley's rescue of the woman and her daughter at the Delaware Water Gap. Apparently, the Pennsylvania State Police had sent an announcement to the paper, and a reporter had come up one day after school to talk to Riley. Riley had given most of the credit to Sam, but he had been pleased when the article appeared to read Sam's description of his own contribution.

"I never congratulated you," Mary said.

"It's no big deal," Riley said, looking down at his feet.

"Yes, it is," his mother said. "But we won't embarrass you further by drawing any more attention to it." She laughed at Riley's blush.

The next day after school, Riley called Sam. It was the first time he had called Sam since the furnace went out and one of the few times he had spoken with Sam since they had returned from Gettysburg two weeks earlier. Sam had told Riley's mother that he was busy finishing a set of cupboards to explain why he wasn't coming around, but Riley wondered if there were other reasons.

"I have to make a chessboard fast," Riley told Sam.

"A chessboard?" Sam asked. "What for? What happened to the one your mother gave you?"

"Nothing," said Riley, "it's fine. But Mary needs one. They're good luck."

Sam laughed. "We'll see what we can do. Be ready in half an hour. I'll pick you up."

Riley spent almost every evening for the next two weeks out at Sam's. Sometimes, when they went into the cabin to get a scrap of something or other, or to have a bowl of ice cream, the odor of paint and turpentine was so strong that he almost gagged. He knew even without going into the studio that Sam had been painting again.

One night, after they had been cutting wood until their noses were filled with sawdust, Sam challenged Riley to a game of chess.

Pawn. Pawn. Pawn. Bishop. Knight. Pawn. Rook. Queen. Bishop.

Riley won eventually, but the game lasted forty-five minutes, and he was down to two pieces at the end.

"Not bad," Riley admitted as they picked up the pieces.

Sam looked at him and, for the first time since they'd met, his eyes twinkled.

Sam taught Riley how to work with wood. The workshop behind the cabin hummed in the evening with the sound of the saw biting its way through strips of walnut and maple. The air grew thick with dust, and the sharp smell of freshly cut wood bit into their nostrils. The gluing went quickly, but the sanding was endless.

"Listen to your hands," Sam said.

"What's that supposed to mean?" Riley asked irritably. His hands and arms ached, and he just wanted it to be done.

"It means your hands will tell you when the wood is smooth enough," Sam explained.

Riley thought that moment would never come, but finally he could run his hands over the wood, and it felt as smooth as Cassie had felt after her baths when she crawled into his lap.

The varnish was thick and golden. It went on like syrup and froze the grain of the wood as if it were God's own artwork on display.

Some days he barely had a minute to himself between school, homework, extra meetings of the chess club, and his regular appointment with Sam. He no longer took Sam's chessboard to school. Instead, Mr. Aja, Mary, and he played on Mr. Aja's set, the one from the discount store. It was silly, and they knew it. They all knew it had nothing whatever to do with the board, but Mary started winning again. Not every game, but many of them. Enough, anyway, to make her laugh when she played.

"Are you sure you don't want to compete?" Mr. Aja asked Riley. "I was very sincere when I said months ago that we would love to add you to our vast roster."

"I'm positive," Riley lied. In truth, he very much wanted the chance to go along with Mr. Aja and Mary to Burlington. Burlington was the biggest city in the state. It had restaurants and shopping centers and movie theaters, all the things that Stony Point had and Sharon didn't, even if he didn't miss them nearly as much anymore as he once had. But more than that, he didn't want to compete against Mary at the tournament or stand in her way.

"Well, then, just come along for the day," Mr. Aja suggested. "You can be the cheering section. Get your feet wet for next year."

"Really?" Riley asked. "Can I do that?"

"I say you can. I'm the chess team coach, the team driver, the official buyer of post-tournament ice cream cones," said Mr. Aja. "What I say goes. Be here at seven-thirty Saturday morning."

He was and Mary was, but Mr. Aja wasn't. They waited, watching the dew on the grass glitter in the slanting morning light. They were both dressed for the warm day to come, not the chill of the early morning. Riley found himself shifting his weight from one foot to the other in a little dance to stay warm.

"I have something for you," Riley said, when he couldn't hold his surprise any longer. He rummaged around in the duffel he'd brought to carry his lunch and raincoat, and brought out his gift, wrapped in newspaper. Immediately, he was embarrassed and wished he could take it back. What if she didn't like it? What if she thought it meant more than it did? He wanted to pull it back and bury it again in his duffel.

"What is it?" she asked, taking it from him.

"Nothing," he told her. He wished Mr. Aja would show up right then and order them into the car.

She gasped when she unwrapped it.

"It's Sam's chessboard!" she said, looking quickly up at him. "This is yours."

"No, it's yours," Riley said with relief. She liked it. He could tell. "Sam helped me make it. It's for good luck."

"You know I can't use it in the tournament," she said anxiously. "You have to use their sets."

"You won't need it," Riley said. "You'll knock their socks off."

And she very nearly did. At the end of the day, Mary went up to get a red ribbon for second place for seventh grade for the entire state of Vermont.

"Even better than last year," Mr. Aja crowed on the way home in the car. True to his word, he swung into the Dairy Queen and treated them all to black raspberry ice cream cones. "And you, Mr. Griffin, deserve some of this splendiferous credit."

"Me? Why?" asked Riley, who didn't need any other reasons to feel good. He had had a wonderful day.

"Because you came along at just the right time to give Mary someone to practice with. I let you slide this year, but you have talent yourself. Next year, I expect you to pull your own weight on this team," he announced. With that, he rolled down the window and started singing, *"God didn't make little green apples, and it don't rain in Indianapolis in the summertime,"* at the top of his lungs.

❧ *Chapter* SIXTEEN

On the Friday before Memorial Day weekend, Riley learned that he was expected, along with every other student who attended the Sharon Consolidated School, to appear Monday morning at nine-thirty for the annual parade through town. Every student would be given a small American flag, and they would all climb the hill behind the school to the cemetery. There they would plant the flags on the graves of the town's veterans from every war in honor of their contributions and sacrifice.

"I had forgotten all about that tradition," his mother said when he told her that night over dinner. "I did it every year. And I was older than you are before I felt anything other than cheated for having to report to school on a national holiday."

Riley understood how she felt when she came in to wake him Monday morning.

"Rise and shine," she said. "Breakfast in ten minutes. It's gray and cool out, so dress warmly."

"Is Sam coming to the parade?" Riley asked.

"No, honey," his mother said gently. "This isn't Sam's holiday."

The organizers had their hands full bringing order to the three hundred children milling about on the sidewalk and street in front of the firehouse. Teachers went around handing out small American flags on staffs the size of knitting needles. Tim Ferris and his goon friends starting fencing with their flags. Someone showed up driving a big white convertible with the roof down. To Riley's surprise Mr. St. Francis was perched alone on the top of the back seat. The town's hero, he wore his army dress uniform, although it no longer buttoned clear down the front, and his cap was cocked on his head. His Purple Heart was pinned to his chest. His eyes were clear and his back was straight. He looked ahead, turning his head neither right nor left, as though no one else were there. The car took its place at the head of the procession.

At ten o'clock, a sheriff's car pulled out into the main street to block traffic and turned on its blue lights. The Sharon school band, which had been warming up, shattering the morning with awkward honks and squeaks, gradually found the correct notes and tempo, and took up a march. The long thin line of students, led by the kindergartners, stepped off under the lowering sky.

Sharon was only three blocks long from the firehouse to the school, and the parade lasted no more than fifteen minutes. Almost everyone in town was there, stretched out, one person deep, the entire length of the route.

Most of the kids behaved themselves. Even the little kids seemed to realize that although this was a parade, it had a somber purpose. At the end, the children unraveled in the schoolyard, and the townspeople who had been following behind, gathered up like iron filings to a magnet, crowded around the school flagpole. The band played "The Star-Spangled Banner," and the piercing treble of one trumpet soared above the rest of the instruments, filling the air with a sound so sweet that Riley could practically taste it. Almost everyone put their hands over their hearts while the band played, but Mr. St. Francis, standing front and center, raised his right hand to his forehead in a stiff salute.

Afterward, the children climbed the stubby hill behind the school and swarmed like ants over the cemetery looking for the small cast-iron stars that marked the graves of veterans everywhere. Riley had not been in the cemetery before, and he was surprised to find stars marking graves from every war in the country's past, from the Revolutionary War to the Civil War to the Spanish-American War to both world wars to the Korean War. One star, not weathered enough yet to have lost all its luster, marked the grave of the single young man from Sharon who had died in Vietnam. Someone who still missed him had obviously come up early in the morning and laid a spray of lilacs near the stone.

Twice Riley was so startled by what he found that he

stopped in his tracks. The first time was when he came across the stone that read JAMES JENNISON, 1840–1903. It had never occurred to him that James Jennison had actually come home to Sharon in his tattered uniform after the war and all the killing, and made a life for himself in this small town. Sarah's stone was next to her husband's, and beside that was a small stone marking the grave of a child, John Jennison, who died in 1870, when he was only one. Just about the same age as Cassie, Riley thought. Riley would have planted his flag next to Jennison's iron star, but two other students had already beaten him to it. He wondered if they were descendants of Jennison's or if they had merely been the first to come across the grave.

A little farther on, he gasped. There were his grand-mother's and grandfather's graves: Wallace and Lily Long. He knew they were buried here—his mother had some-times said she was going to visit their graves—but he had never made the trip, short as it was. He was just as shocked to stumble across their graves as he was by the iron star at the side of his grandfather's headstone. For service in World War II, it said. Riley was astonished. He didn't know his grandfather had fought in World War II. His mother had never mentioned it. He was considering putting his flag on his grandfather's grave, even though there were already half a dozen flags planted there and fluttering feebly in the light breeze, when Mary and Claire came up beside him.

"I didn't know my grandfather fought in World War II," Riley told them, pointing at the iron star.

They were shivering in their jackets.

"Where did you put your flag?" he asked Mary. He was new to this, and he wondered if there was any logic to this tradition.

Mary held up her hand to show him that she still had hers.

"I always give mine to my dad," she explained. "And he never throws them away. He keeps them all in his top drawer."

✂ ✂ ✂

Within half an hour everyone had dispersed. Riley drifted home to find Sam's truck parked in the driveway.

"I didn't know Grandpa fought in World War II," Riley said as he came into the kitchen, where Sam and his mother were talking.

"Well, he didn't really," his mother explained. "He was too old to fight, but they needed all the able-bodied men they could find. He had a desk job."

"You get an iron star for sitting at a desk?" Riley asked in disbelief.

"There are all kinds of ways to serve your country," she replied. "And all of them have value."

"Come on, Riley," Sam said, standing up and stretching his lanky frame like a cat that has been sleeping too long. "Guess what I have. A pane of glass from an old house I've been tearing down that we can use to replace that awful piece of new glass in the dining room window. Help me put it in."

Without waiting for Riley to answer, Sam headed out the door, and Riley had no choice but to follow.

They had done the hard work in the fall. Now they quickly pried the window from its frame and laid it on the grass. It took Sam only a minute to remove the glazing and new glass and slip the old piece of glass into place.

Carefully, Riley helped tamp the new glazing around the fragile pane. Then Sam held up the window high between them so they could admire it. Once again, all nine panes matched in a crazy fashion. Riley could see the flowing curves and pinpoint bubbles of trapped air in the old glass, the kind of distortions that Sam said changed the way you saw the world.

He looked at Sam through the panes. It struck him that the old window broke Sam into pieces, the way the war had broken him, and then put him back together imperfectly, just the way he had been trying to put his life back together since returning to Sharon. Not everything lined up. It never would. He wasn't any different from Mr. St. Francis or James Jennison, whose lives had been broken by their principles, and who had come home to try to piece their lives together again.

"Don't you think," Riley asked suddenly, "that if you

tell your country you think it is doing the wrong thing, that you are still serving your country?"

Sam lowered the window.

"Sometimes it's the most patriotic thing you can do," Sam said. "But you won't get any medals for it."

"That doesn't seem fair," Riley said.

"Almost nothing about war is fair. But that's the way it is," Sam said.

Riley held the window in place while Sam hammered the frame back together.

"Come on," Sam said, "let's go have some of your mother's pea soup."

Walking back into the house, warming his hands in the pockets of his jacket and listening to Sam's soft voice as Sam told him about a doe and a speckled fawn he had seen just after dawn in the woods behind his cabin, Riley felt the flag he had been given that morning still curled like a fist around its thin staff.

At the top of the steps, before they crossed the porch and went into the bright, warm kitchen, Riley stopped. He pulled the flag out and shook it loose.

"Here," he said, handing it to Sam. "This is for you."

Nancy Price Graff has published three nonfiction books for children with Little, Brown and a picture book, *In the Hush of the Evening*, with HarperCollins. *A Long Way Home* is her first novel. Ms. Graff lives in Montpelier, Vermont.